■PEOPLE LIVE STILL IN
CASHTOWN CORNERS

TONY BURGESS

ChiZine Publications

FIRST EDITION

LIBRARY AND ARCHIVES CANADA CATALOGUING IN PUBLICATION

Burgess, Tony, 1959-
    People live still in Cashtown Corners / Tony Burgess.

ISBN 978-1-926851-05-1

    I. Title.

PS8553.U63614P46 2010   C813'.54   C2010-903995-5=20

CHIZINE PUBLICATIONS
Toronto, Canada
www.chizinepub.com
info@chizinepub.com

Edited by Brett Alexander Savory
Copyedited and proofread by Sandra Kasturi

 Canada Council   Conseil des Arts
for the Arts   du Canada

We acknowledge the support of the Canada Council for the Arts which last year invested $20.1 million in writing and publishing throughout Canada.

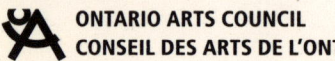 ONTARIO ARTS COUNCIL
CONSEIL DES ARTS DE L'ONT.

Published with the generous assistance of the Ontario Arts Council.

PEOPLE LIVE STILL IN
CASHTOWN CORNERS

For Rachel Jones, my true love

■1

There is a point at which you find yourself, where, and this is not just what I think but this is the way we are designed to think and it's this: if the entire universe, and I mean every corner of every atomized corner of infinity; if everything that is isn't aware of or doesn't understand my most inconsequential, half-formed thoughts, then there is no chance that the highest-formed acts by the noblest mind are greater than gross self-love.

When I scrape tar from the side of my sneakers onto the edge of the island, it passes through the world as both the idea that preceded me doing it but also as a shadow formed by my shoe leaning edgewise, and it forms a commanding ripple outward through all things. It must be exactly this way or the little hand that saves the little face from drowning in a great flood somewhere else is the same as shitting. I exist in an infinite number of times.

I stand beside the island, all of my transforming eyes moving independently, sure; but primarily I swing my arms in a natural way as I approach a car pulled over at Cashtown Corners. It is a silver 2005 Corolla with a single occupant. She is leaning over to examine her purse and positioning her head so that she can see through the side mirror. I am aware of when she can see me and this is one of the primary recordings. We are both aware of the recordings being made as I stop at her window. She will pause for a broken second to appear natural—it is a theatrical device; if you are interrupted it gives the illusion you aren't pretending. Her hand stops between her purse and the stick and she looks ahead before looking up.

"Fill, please. Regular."

I don't smile and turn toward the back

of the car. This is just going to be what I call a nothing. That is, I am not going to do anything with this. The gas door pops open as she releases it from within and I pull it back and twist off the cap. There will be a dark belly inside the car waiting for this moment but I will act as if all I care about is what I do next. The nozzle is taken from the pump. The grade is selected and the nozzle is inserted into the fitted hole. The hose jerks up a little when the gas enters. So, as you can see, I am fully capable of acting as if everything is going to matter. I don't know how much gas she will need and I am willing to accept that this is still going to be all right. I step away from the pump. She looks at this and I move to her window. Am I caught up in something now? Are things— very distant things, mind you—lifting their heads above the grass to 'get involved'? I can't say. It's not exactly that kind of thing.

"Clean your windshield?"

One expects that I am aware how old-fashioned it is to ask this, to do this kind of courtesy. I am not aware of this, even as I point it out. I am aware, however, that she has smiled and has nodded pleasantly. I draw the squeegee, even as I resent the word, out of the bucket. Water is carried in the form of a comet tail up to her windshield.

She looks uncomfortable as I work the sponge side in small wobbles across the white 'R' of a flattened insect. She doesn't want to look up at it. I am aware that to her it's as if I had removed my penis from my pants and pushed its tip onto the surface of her eye. Its eye and her eye touching. She looks down at her knees. I have taken the insect away but left a chalk outline. The same as cliché activists leave behind. I do see the 'T' of the squeegee as a shade and I decide that, except for this woman breaking piss tears on her cheek, things are very 'this happens all the time now.' I do put the 'T' shadow and the 'R' insect aside in case today is a special word as well.

She cranes back to see the pump through the rear passenger window. She pretends to read it and looks to me for the number she has just pretended to read.

"Thirty-two."

She acts pleased and gives me two twenties.

As her Corolla leaves the lot the rear drops and bounces up. I always watch for this. I'm not sure why. The car turns and sits at the red light. This is one of my favourite things. Cashtown Corners is an intersection at the bottom of a small but deep basin. You drop to get here and you climb to leave. It's a very descriptive place to be. And most of the time there is no one here but me. I have sat and watched lights turn red, then green, then orange, then red, then green, then orange, then red, then green, then orange and on and on without a single car or truck or person to see it. She sits at the red light, as dumb as the air around her, and waits. I watch and I am the air around her now. The light turns green. It doesn't just turn green. A chuck of darkness drops in the way of the red and the green rises. These are the moments I watch. I want to see their character. The car will not move instantly. It will sit for a moment and then move. In that second I look for what the car says. Each car that accepts a colour and acts does so in the form of talking. These are some that I have heard: "Oh, I was going to go now anyway so thanks for reminding me," and "Thank heavens it's time to go," and "I'm not sure—I should look, but you know," and "I have only ever glanced at you to see if we agree on things." The woman in the silver Corolla sits for a while at the green. I always enjoy this kind. She sits in front of the green light and doesn't move. No car but hers for as far as the eye can see.

I step from my booth and walk toward her. It's so weird because I don't really have an expectation, but because she has not moved on a green and we sit at the bottom of an empty dirt and gravel satellite dish in the country, we can experiment with the basic assumptions. As I approach her car I see what she is doing. She is applying makeup or something. Some light thing at the front of her face. She sees me coming and stops.

I stop. Here we are like two long shadows, minute hands and hour hands cutting into a black and white city. I lift my arm and point to the green light. She is going to play this a little different than you or I might. Roll down the window. Don't roll down the window. Put the mascara away to talk to the man or just wave with it. Smile face or cry face? She has opted for cry face and wave at the man. I turn my point into an upturned hand and the light goes green to orange.

The light goes green to orange.

The light. Goes. Green. To. Orange.

I am not a sentimental man. I'm not a particularly empathetic man. But the light has gone from green to orange and she waits. But the light had been green and now it has gone. That particular interval of green that had been waiting in a throat like the only word ever spoken. The only word that had a hope of pushing aside the tongue. Of treating the meat of the mouth to a brief second of real dancing. And she sat while the mouth crashed like a stricken child and while the ear of these corners, the ears themselves, sharp and perfectly cut to match and vanish—she sat and made her little cry face at me while the ears disappeared.

She doesn't expect me to open her door, and let me set this up properly for you. A lone car sits at a perfectly good intersection in the bottom of a basin. A man has left his booth on the lot where she has just bought gas. The man approaches her car and points. She looks annoyed and a little surprised. He then walks up to her vehicle and opens the door. He says something to her and she tries to close the door but he has pulled it open even farther. She pushes down on the gas to escape but he has a very tight hold of her arm. The car moves into the middle of the intersection but she slides to the ground still held by the hook of the man's hand.

The car rolls to an edge of the intersection, then up into a pile of stones.

The woman tries to escape. She's kicking the ground and swinging at the man with her free hand but he has a very tight hold of her arm. The man gets the woman onto her back and he steps on her neck. You can see him bouncing all his weight on the one foot. She soon stops moving and he quickly drags her back up onto the lot and past his little booth. Just before they enter the trailer at the back of the lot she moves again. Her hands make grabby gestures at the ground, but he manages with a series of kicks to get her safely into the trailer.

I have seen the whole world appear green. I have seen the whole world appear red.

One of the things I like to do while I sit in my booth is pretend it's September 11. How awesome is that? Anyone can do it and it's like you have the greatest time for free. Your imagination can do whatever it wants to, of course, and that's how we get things like sex with alligators and people who make baby bridges across rivers of lava. But every once in a while the imagination gets to step over its borders and be something. That happened on September 11. An airplane going several hundred miles an hour, full of people, pierced the side of a building. I like to think about looking out the window of the plane. Oh. Look. There's New York City rising up around me. Buildings so close it looks like the wings are touching them. There's a gentleness to the wings. They are flexible and stretch up slightly as we descend. They are compensating a little, controlling the air flow, making certain that the pressure above the wings is lighter than that below. And the buildings seem to lean slightly away to make room. This flight plan, this design, this cityscape is commercial. Business is done this way. People have to feel secure in order to buy things, to invest their money. We have bought these tickets to ride in order to get places. You see how you think? You are drawing together all the comfort that design has implied and you are stretching your legs and waiting for the chance to stand and walk away.

Then the nose of the plane touches the side of the building. It doesn't wait there but if we'd like, it can. The plane's nose touches the building like a baby whale floats to its mother's side and pushes its nose against to her as if to say, "I'm here, mom." The plane is perpendicular to the building. The building is immovable and sunk into the only footprint it will ever make. It is so tall, though, that it takes on some of the air's properties. The illusion that it moves, that it soars, that it rises. The plane, which now waits quietly, still touching the building, has in fact some of the air's properties and this isn't an illusion.

You sit forward in your chair a little, trying to relieve a knot at the base of your back. The edge of the building the plane has touched is visible through your window and you see the sun reflected like a giant diamond. Big things are only beautiful because they are big. They may in fact be ugly and small and poorly imagined. The nose of the plane turns up and crinkles as if that was all it intended to do. An instinctive expression. A bothered face that says something. But the eyes and the mouth and forehead enter an office space where several people sit and stand amid desks and cubicles. They ignore the plane that is now a number of feet in. It tightens its jaw and pulls the floor down. I can see someone at a photocopier, which means I am inside now. I am standing inside a plane inside a building. There are food and clothes in the air. There are shoulders compensating. There are wheels on sticks meeting at angles. You have ways of knowing this is happening, but it's frustrating. It's like an infection you have. You know you have it. The skin burns a little and you have more emotion than you know what to do with, but when you ask the doctor, "Is it spreading?" and he says, "This will stop it," he hasn't really answered your questions. You want to know what the infection is doing.

It advances in tissue. It colours and corrupts cells. It multiplies, giving birth over and over again inside you, splashing into your eyes and lungs. So you wanted to know: How many advance? How much dies? Doctor's guess. They sit at the bottom of a dish and study the lights. When you slip down the side they will tell you to wait for the green, but what they don't tell you is that they know absolutely nothing and that the lights change whether he says so or not or whether you are there or not.

The plane goes in and it's just September 11. Soon another one will come and it's still September 11.

■ 2

I have to go to town this morning. I'll tell you later about what happened with me and that lady. Right now I gotta go into town to get some stuff. I have a boy who does a short shift from four in the afternoon until eight. He's a really nice kid. Jeremy. He lives with his parents in Creemore. I don't think it's easy for kids these days. Especially in small towns. There are all kinds of pressures on you to do bad things and good things. And, let's face it, you're going to have to do a little of both before you level off. Anyhow, Jeremy seems a good kid. Respectful and friendly, but he listens to music and likes his skateboard.

"Hi."

He calls me Mr. Clark sometimes, but not this afternoon.

"Hey, Jeremy."

He sets his skateboard behind the windshield washer fluid.

"Pump three is really slow for some reason so I'm trying to avoid it. If the fuel truck comes this afternoon you can mention it to him and he might ask about it for me."

He nods, but I know he won't mention it. It's okay. I pull my till out and slide it into the safe and pull out his.

He checks his pen and the things he likes around, like his watch which he lays out beside the till and a little MP3 player he plugs into my boombox. He doesn't start this all up until I go. Kids like to live in their own world but the good ones wait until you're gone first.

We don't talk much and for a moment I stand thinking about this. Should we? Is something missing from this? I have said I like him and given some good reasons. I saw how he liked his possessions and I fixed him up with his own till. He is aware that I'm just standing here.

"Anything else, Mr. Clark?"

See? I told you he calls me Mr. Clark. I can't answer him right away because obviously I'm thinking about how I had said this and I'm just holding on until I stop thinking about it.

"Is it okay if I listen to music?"

See? I told you that he likes music. Unfortunately the things he's saying and doing are such strong reminders of what I have been saying that it's a bit like I'm in two places at once. He's looking at me but he can't figure it out, either. I am going to have to do something that I have not been thinking about. I turn and leave.

I manage to get out the door but stop beside pump one. I guess it feels like I should just go back in there and say something only to him. I can sense him looking. I raise my hand and say, "Going to town." He waves back but can't hear me. It feels a little sad that we are talking like this. Time to go.

East of Cashtown Corners is Creemore.

West is nothing really, unless you push through to New Lowell. South is Avening. North is Stayner. The truck I get into is a 1972 Chevrolet pickup. I won it three years ago at the Stayner Lion's Club 37th Annual Summer Dance and Truck draw. The damn thing is cherry red. I never take it to Stayner for obvious reasons. I opt instead for Creemore.

"How can I help you today, Mr. Clark?"

That's Jeffrey Peck or Feck or something. The pharmacist. Tough little guy. Looks like a champion thumb wrestler. Mean and thick and strong. I don't like faces on people in town so I scribble over them. I don't actually recall what Feck looks like in the face. Just swirls and loops out of a ball point. Round and round and round. When he talks, two or three blue wires vibrate horribly. Doesn't make me want to answer.

"Gotta headache, Mr. Clark?"

He's talking to me like I'm a kid so I head for the door. Penny Larkin is on the cash. She tries to smile at me but the tangle of blue lines that make up her head only manage to sort of point around the room in a random way.

"Need some gum."

Penny's head stops for moment.

"Well, there's lots of gum. They come out with a new kind of gum every day."

This isn't precisely what I had in mind when I came to town. I didn't want gum. I'm merely trying to get outside now. But before I leave I'm going to get this right. If I am just about anything I want to be and I can be that thing just about anywhere I want, how is it that I can get trapped like this? At the back of the store I'm supposed to know about a headache. Up here, standing within a foot or two of the door, I need to be thinking about what it means to make new gum everyday. This question about gum is the one that has problems. A new gum every day. I can feel that that might be horrible. It almost sounds as if we are giving up other things to allow this. I am staring at a pyramid of jaw harp boxes. Aware that there is no obvious or clear path through this. I can't tell how badly Penny needs me right now. The gum doesn't matter to us. I touch the top jaw harp box. Pale yellow with Halloween-orange writing. I should not have put the scribbles on her face.

"That's what ya need? A jaw harp?"

I picture Penny lifting the jaw harp to her face. The vicious bramble of lines. Two or three purse outward and the harp is caught up like a mouse in the talons of a hawk.

Outside I put the jaw harp in my top pocket. I pat the pocket and the box is a perfect fit. I feel Penny watching my back as I walk. I can't believe she almost made me cry.

The truck is parked behind the Foodland. I have to get something other than the jaw harp or Jeremy'll think I'm nuts. I can get bread and stuff. I feel that sandwiches will be made, but I have this terrible feeling in my head they are already made. It's a common feeling. You make a plan to do something and it sits in your mind as a thing you've already done. Then when you act, there is the awful pulling apart of things that belong to specific moments. It is often impossible to act, to stay clear. I step out onto the parking lot in front of the Foodland but before I get past the first parked car I am struck by a sharp smell. I recognize it and you have probably smelled it yourself. It is the smell of your emotions. When things aren't going well, like today, that smell hits me and I feel like I'm in grade two and my mother has dropped me off late for school and it's raining and I'm standing against the wall unable to go in. The smell. When you're an adult those little childish boxes that come up around you can almost prevent you from breathing. I have to stop walking, actually stop walking, and hold my nose so I breathe only through my mouth. But smell is unlike your other senses. Sight and sound are all about wavelengths and receptors. Smell is about the particle itself. Some of the thing you are thinking has to enter your head. When you smell someone's urine, that means some of the urine itself has travelled into your head and is resting there. So this smell now, triggered by me having to imagine the sandwich not made and holding up the bricks of a school, has removed some of these events, molecules of them, the tiny vibrating beads of them and crammed them up my nasal cavity. I need to blow my nose. Even though the smell has faded, those things are still lying in there. They have already created a new unreliable memory out of this trip to Creemore and it should have been so simple. I had to buy some oil.

Oil. That's what I'm here for. Not sandwiches or gum or jaw harps. I need to get some oil. So I'll say briefly what is happening then I'll buy some oil. I have had a bad moment followed by a fairly good one. I should be just walking off and shaking my head a little then going to get the twelve cans of oil. I will do that, because I described it so breezily; however, and this is a big however: what am I to make of some of these other difficulties? I'm reasonable, I'm out in front of the problem, which is fine except that, when this happens, when I feel I'm out in front and going to do something, I become overcome by the sensation that I have died. I feel actual grief. Who I am is dead and that's the problem I am now out in front of. So really, how happy can I possibly be? Ever?

"Bin there, done that."

Lilly. Three-hundred-and-fifty-pound woman with a bright red cone for a head. I can't look at her.

"Hey, Bob. Remember when Keith's wife said she was gonna be a reasonable human being?"

I go to put my heavy bags down on the pavement so we can have this chat, but I realize too late that I don't have any bags. She's the one with the bag. So I'm leaning down with my hands heavy at the end of my arms and I touch my toes. I'm stretching. It's been a while.

"You okay? Anyway, she's not. Being a human being, I mean. She is such a bitch and she made all this noise last fall about how while this divorce was going on she was gonna be a grown up and she didn't want to hurt the children and they're the most important thing in all this, but I said to Keith, I says, you watch, she's saying that now but the person she is is gonna come flyin' out in flyin' colours once you have to start deciding serious things, and Keith's all like, no mom, she's really trying this time, and well, look, hey, she's turning the kids against him and saying he's lazy and even saying that he hits them. Well, she was the one hitting them when they didn't deserve it. There's all this stuff every day now about how you should hit kids when they're this tall but not when they're this tall and wait, no, when they're this age and not—you know when you hit a kid? You know when you hit a kid? When the kid's gone too far and is being a little fucker and knows it and knows that you know he's being a little fucker. You just know as a parent. Parents know, but she's now all of a sudden been reading up on studies and reports and she thinks she knows exactly how he messed up those kids. So I says to him, I says, the day you let her get under your skin was the day you lost this battle. Cause he did. He did hit her and that's something he has to face up to and whether she deserved it or not that's just not how the world works once you get police and courts and lawyers involved. I told him, I said, now you have to live your whole goddam life as if you're defending it in front of a judge. Since when did everybody have to decide what's right for everybody? It's sad though, Bob, it breaks my heart to see him like this. He can't be a husband any more and now I don't see how he can be a father. And why? What's the reason?"

I don't know why she has a red cone for a head while everyone else in town has scribbles for heads.

"Anyway, we're letting him stay with us for a while. I've never seen anyone get so low so fast. It breaks my heart. And those kids, well, Sheila's still a little sweetie but that Paula is a monster from hell. She's her mother. And that's gonna be a big problem. But, anyway, so, we have our own things we're dealing with aside from all this other stuff. My sister had her tubal finally and she's doing okay, except she just gobbled up her pain meds in the first couple of days. I don't know if she was taking four or five at a time but those things are hard to get. Oxycontin. Your doctor has to make arrangements with the pharmacy cause they don't have that stuff lying around any more. So she's out of her Oxy's and if I have to hear her whine about it one more time when she knows full well that you have to pace yourself with that stuff especially when you got this humungous scar running across your belly and your insides all yanked out. Yes, it's going to hurt but it's up to you to be responsible, you can't just take those things like that. I think she was getting high. That's what I think, but she doesn't say that. She'd never admit it. She's a mom now and has two teenagers so all that stuff is behind her. Well, newsflash if you're eating four or five Oxycontin every four or five hours then you're pretty much acting the exact same way as when you were a kid drinking wine and doing acid out by the reservoir. In fact I bet she does know what she's doing. I bet she's pretty sure that she can get more of those Oxy's. Anyway, I got other things to worry about. All my fish died in the pond. Didn't last the winter. Don't know if it was too cold and froze right to the bottom or maybe they didn't get enough food. Who knows? All I know is they're supposed to survive the winter or I wouldn't have left them out there. I'm heartbroken and I don't know how to tell the kids. They named the fish last summer. But not gonna have to worry about it cause if the bitch gets her way I won't ever see my grandchildren again. So, that's one less thing to worry about. How are you? You gotta sore back?"

I look at her.

"No? Well, here give me a hand getting these bags into the van."

She drops the bags and pulls out her keys.

At the van she slides the side door open. I push her in and fall on top of her.

I hold her down with all my weight. Her back is wide and soft but she's still pretty strong and does a push-up. I'm surprised she hasn't yelled yet. I pull her arms out flattening her and I put my knees on her shoulder blades. She takes a bunch of fast breaths and before she can do anything with all that oxygen I punch the back of her head. She collapses a little and I have a chance to pull the seat belt across and under her throat. I can't get it to loop around so I just pull hard under her chin. Now she won't yell for sure. I put a knee on the back of her neck and haul up hard on the belt. This is pretty much gonna be it for a while. I hold and pull hard, not moving or letting her move. When she does move a little I take advantage and draw the belt tighter under her chin. This is how snakes do it. When the prey breathes or tries to escape, the snake tightens. If you never let up and keep applying the pressure, things just kill themselves eventually. She rocks a little now, but again that's just working to fully close her windpipe. Finally she has exhaled and can't inhale. She bucks under me and tries to turn to one side. I see her face now. The red cone has fallen away, but her cheek is speckled with crimson. The white of the eye is clouding up pink. She stiffens and I just keep the pressure on. I'm pretty sure that's it for her but I hold on for a while. That's it. Sweat is falling from my face like cluster flies down a cold winter window. The drops bomb her back and stain her shirt. I sit up on her and lean back to swing the door shut. In the dark I move my legs down, wiggling my hips to the flatter part of her back where it's more comfortable. I guess I'm waiting for something. While I was killing her I felt pretty sure I was completely losing control of myself. I thought that once she died I was going to just start pulling her body apart and filling the whole van with blood and guts. I even thought that I'd eat some of her and cover myself in gore. It's a feeling that got hold of me and carried right through to the finish. But now I sit here on top of her and I am definitely not going to do any of that. If pushed I wouldn't object to it but the wild need of it seems to have just calmly stepped aside. I sit on her. Her warm sides fill the floor around me and I feel very comfortable. My mind isn't snapped or anything. I'm not particularly afraid of what I've done even though I do know that now, whatever happens, at some point down the road I'm going to have to listen to someone tell me what I've done. That isn't a very nice thought; however it isn't what's happening now. I am sitting on her soft body and I stay like this for quite a while.

Later I pull the bags off the asphalt and into the van. I lie along her side with an elbow resting on the fat across her spine and I go through the bags. Roast Chicken Chips. Two large bags, a deli box of potato wedges, a six pack of Kool-Aid Jammers, a narrow box of thirty large freezer bags. Some lean ground beef. A packet of Bahai Citrus Marinade. Two large plastic bottles of Coke Zero. As I pull these things out of the bags I lay them on and around her. Not for any special reason, just so I can get a look at what she bought. Some pink deodorant. I check. Anti-perspirant. The difference preoccupies me for a moment. Two cans of beans with lard. And, a little surprising, a very large pair of purple Crocs. Not real Crocs. Foodland Crocs. I look at the plastic loop that holds them together. This, I decide, is where I'll focus. I have decided that even though I'm not feeling bad, in fact, better than I have all morning, I need to conjure some emotion to commemorate the event. The Crocs she will never wear. The plastic loop she'll never pull across her teeth to break. That's the poignant thing. These rubbery shoes she'll never work her toes into. It must be so sad. I hold them for a moment. They are so light it feels as though they would float if I let go of them. I turn the tag over. Doesn't say much. A bar code. A price. $5.99. Size 11. I hold my mouth closed in case

I cry, but I feel a broad smile in my hand. The fake Crocs she will never gnaw apart. I have to admit to myself that there is no way to feel genuinely bad about this. I sit up to see if I feel any burden. I don't and realize that that's probably just as bad as if I had ripped her apart and eaten her. I feel good, but it's not that simple. Something very dangerous, something far worse than what has happened just now has been put out of service. We enter into battles without understanding the terms of our survival and when we do survive, when we do what is necessary, when we pull up strong, then all the rest, this cost, this remainder of my life, is only lessened because we did so much more than all the others. We stood while God hammered the sky and we never stopped walking while chainsaws milked our legs and we did something very wrong and awful, but at least it cleared the air. It lifts those that come after. It was us we offered up and no one will ever know this but us.

I think I'm okay with this now. I do feel bad

after all. She didn't really deserve to die and I didn't really have to kill her. But this is what hands have done and this is how we move on. I reach back and pull the doors open and step out of the van.

The sun is brilliant, turning the light grey parking lot into a white hot bath. I step away, my head lowered, not crazed or frantic or covert. In fact, I have her Crocs in my hand.

One of the things Creemore likes about itself is the names of the two rivers that run up either side. The Mad and the Noisy. Much is made of these two rivers' names. There's a Mad and Noisy Art Gallery. Other things. There's a micro brewery that draws water from the Mad and Noisy. All that would be fine, because there's no denying the fun, but the entire population of the town seems to think they're mad and noisy because of this. And some of them have a kind of mad and noisy affectation. I swear. It's hard to put your finger on, exactly, but you can see it. A little sunken in the eyes, a little wild in the hair, and all sparkly talking. I think about the effect a place's name can have on people. I am the only person who lives at Cashtown Corners. Should I have a lot of cash? Not much you can do about that. Although, it has occurred to me that people often pay cash for their gas. Most people use plastic to pay for gas anyway for sure. I actually think more about Johnny Cash when it comes to Cashtown. I mean, if a town in Alberta called Vulcan can claim to be Spock's birthplace and erect statues and serve ham and live-long-and-prosper eggs, and give Leonard Nimoy the keys to the town in a big parade, then—no. It's pretty clear you're a fool if you think the names of places make you something. Cashtown.

I pick up my oil. Buy two cases and haul it back up Main Street to where I parked my pickup at the pharmacy. I drop the case in the bed and pat my jaw harp pocket.

Cherry's a silly colour for a pickup, but it was free. I peer into the pharmacy and **wave** to Penny Larkin. She seems to have cheered up a bit so I wave again. As I walk along the side of the truck I spy those purple Crocs. I had tossed them in there on my way to get the oil. A sad little reminder but I suppose I needed one. I reach in and pull them up by the plastic loop. Not every day you can say you got shoes like these to take home. Cone faces and squiggle heads. Good Lord. Not every day.

■ 3

On the drive from Creemore to Cashtown corners, I listen to Barrie's rock station. I only have about five minutes or so and I always hope to hear a good song. It's an old Pink Floyd song. Nice enough. Sort of floaty. Out in a field to the south a tractor drags a wide tiller through dry soil. An orange-brown cloud rolls up into the air behind it and hundreds of seagulls fill the floating dirt. I've heard people say, "Oh, no. The seagulls are eating all the seeds!" That's not what's happening, of course. The farmer is tilling not seeding. The seagulls are eating worms in the turned earth.

I turn up onto the lot and swing around the pumps. A yellow Camry is sitting empty beside pump six. I pause for the person to come out. She does and hops in her Camry. The silver Corolla still sits against the rocks on the northeast corner.

"Hey. There's a Corolla sitting over—"

"I know."

"Should we call the police or someone?"

"Wait a minute. Lemme go check it out."

The keys are still in the ignition and I start it. It rolls back onto the road and I pull it up behind the trailer. A little out of sight. As I'm walking back to the booth I hear a distant siren. The sound sears as the cruisers drop into the basin. Two. Lights flashing in ridiculous combinations as if they're too excited to make sense. I pause, shield my eyes and watch them race through the red light toward Creemore.

"Well, I didn't call 'em."

Jeremy is walking back from having turned his music off.

"Nope. That's some other business."

"You don't see cruisers goin' off like that to Creemore very often."

"Nope. Some big emergency."

I watch Jeremy to see what he thinks.

"I know there's a meth lab in town."

I whistle.

"Really? Well, I bet that's what they're after, then."

"There gonna need hazmat suits."

I nod, agreeing. But really, hazmat suits? I try to picture the meth lab, though I have no idea what a meth lab is supposed to look like. Instead, I picture the van with the dead woman inside.

"What was with the car?"

I can see those seagulls. They wheel around against the ground like a giant saw.

"Car?"

"Yeah. The Corolla. What are we gonna do about that?

"Oh, yeah. Hmmm. Not much we can do."

I keep my eyes on the gulls. I'm aware of what I've just said but have said it in a way that sounds settled. I can see Jeremy out of the corner of my eye. He moves a little, picking something up.

"Didja get the oil?"

I nod but stay focused on the gulls.

"I just think it's kinda weird. A car left like that. It wasn't even parked or anything. Looks like it just rolled up off the road all by itself."

I turn to see what he's picked up. A pen. I'm a little surprised at how nothing much has happened since I got back. I don't even remember exactly how events got so crowded up earlier.

"Oh. Well. I guess we'll find out one way or another."

I smile and Jeremy smiles back, but he looks a little vexed. I think he wants me to say more about this. I could. In fact, right now, the way I'm feeling, I could probably pull off just about any story I cared to tell. It's odd how dramatically things have changed. I think this is a moment I need to seize. I think this is how we turn a corner.

"Okay. Okay. Jeremy?"

"Yeah?"

"Would you like a lot of money?"

Jeremy shrugs. Jeremy's parents have no money. His mom works one shift a week at the vinegar factory and his dad has probably never worked anywhere for very long. Jeremy has no money.

"No. I mean it. Here."

I go over to the big map of Georgian Bay and I lift it from the wall. Jeremy turns slowly. He is a watcher. Probably grew up that way. I enter the combination to the safe and draw the door open.

"Money, Jeremy, money."

I remove a thick envelope and place it on his knee. He looks down then scoops it up before it falls.

"Go ahead. Take a look."

Jeremy peeks in the envelope.

"That's twelve thousand dollars."

"Wow. You should put it back though."

I drag a stool across the floor and sit facing the boy.

"That is money I keep just in case."

"Just in case what?"

"Just in case I need to do something that costs money."

"That's smart. That's a lot of money. That's smart."

"Well, it's mine to do with what I want to do."

Jeremy looks up from the money. He wants to ask something but just takes me in a bit.

"So what I've decided is I want to give it to you."

"Why? What do I have to do?"

Jeremy is holding the envelope out for me to take back.

"Nope. It's yours. I don't need it or want it."

Jeremy returns the envelope to his lap. I give a big smile.

"Can you guess what?"

"No. What?"

I look at his face.

"Follow me."

Jeremy tries to give me back the envelope as we stand but I put my hand over his and push the envelope to his stomach.

He walks behind me past the pumps.

"I bet that car is stolen. That's what it is for sure."

I turn back as we walk and say nothing. We reach the trailer and I try to think of something to say. I can't think of a thing. I have decided to just enjoy this moment. I open the trailer door and step up.

Jeremy comes in behind me. It's not a big space and I have to back between the fridge and counter to let him in. Jeremy looks a little nervous but that's pretty damn normal I'd say. I stretch out my hand to present what he's here to see.

The woman from the silver Corolla lies on the floor alongside the kitchenette. She is face-down and dead. The back of her head is stove in. Her hair is sticking up in black crusty spikes. We stand looking at her for a while. I don't have much to say yet and I can sense that Jeremy won't say anything until I do. So I give it a try.

"Well, that's what I wanted to show you."

I turn to him and he appears unable to take his eyes off her.

"So? What do you think of that?"

Jeremy pulls his stare up and looks at me. I half smile, hedging how I think this is going to turn out.

"It is what it is. That's her car out there and, well, that's her right there."

Jeremy looks at the woman again. There's a few flies dipping in and out of the back of her skull.

"What happened to her?"

I feel a little uncomfortable. I wasn't really planning to lay it all out like this.

"Well, I hate to say this but I killed her."

Jeremy nods slowly. He's starting to take this in and I'm relieved.

"Don't ask me why. Anything I say is just gonna sound ridiculous."

I rub my hand in my hair. I want to appear frustrated.

"Things just got out of control."

Jeremy hasn't moved. He doesn't even appear to be breathing.

"Big time. Anyway. You keep the money, okay?"

Jeremy looks back to me. I cannot figure out what he's thinking. That's what the money's for.

"Oh, don't worry. You don't have to do anything. I'll take care of all this. You just take the money. You need it as much as I do."

I take a deep breath to encourage him to breathe.

"This is all on me. You don't even worry."

I step between Jeremy and the lady and reach across to open the door. He glances up at me then backs out.

"You just forget all about it, okay? That's a lot of money."

I walk beside him toward the booth, then I tap his elbow.

"Wait. I should probably get rid of that car. You mind the pumps. I won't be long."

I wait for Jeremy to say something. I've just given him a lot of money. He should at least say something.

"Okay. I'll be right back."

Jeremy nods. He's acting a bit mechanical. I'm doing very well but I have to keep in mind that there's a shock value. I slap him on the arm and head for the Corolla.

I'm not sure where I'm going to take this car. Wherever I do take it I'm going to have to walk back so it can't be far. I was hoping Jeremy might be willing to give me a ride but I think he doesn't want to get involved. I pull off the lot and wave to Jeremy. He waves back.

I take the road back to Creemore but drive slowly, looking for places to dump the car. The seagulls have settled around the tiller, which now sits idle in the field. I can't just leave it at the side of the road. It'd attract attention pretty much right away. I guess I'm heading back to Creemore. In the rear view I can still see the gas station. There's a big blue Dodge Ram at pump two and Jeremy's hopped out of the booth. I'm trying to figure out if these events have a finish line. If there's some set of actions I can take or ways I can just lay the facts down so they don't move. Some way to keep everybody calm. It's my responsibility. I'm the one who has to live with this.

I turn down Main Street and there's the cruisers at the Foodland. They've cordoned off the van with yellow tape and the Foodland manager is outside. Wonder how they found her so fast? She was the turning point. After her, things just seemed to go a lot smoother. I must be at war or something.

I drive a little past the Foodland and the pharmacy. Past the brewery I turn up to the play park by the church. The car can sit here all day without anyone noticing. People come and go to this park all the time. Walking dogs and kids. You can't know whose car is whose just by looking. You see a car or cars and you move on.

I pull up under the shade of a big maple beside the park. Turn off the ignition and hold the keys. I could ask for a ride back from somebody. The car squawks when I lock it. I toss the keys high into the tree. They tear through leaves then fall just on the other side of the fence. Locked Corolla in the shade and keys on the ground between two exposed roots. Is this a narrative? Try again. *Oh, yeah, there's a locked Corolla parked across from the church. Really? Why are you telling me? Well, because the keys are on the ground just inside the park. What do you think? Somebody dropped them, I guess. What should we do?*

I don't look in on the pharmacy. I really feel like talking to someone and Penny's a good person, but there's things hanging out in the open now that I can't get caught with. I pass the fountain with the statues of shoeless kids in the water and I stop. Sometimes you just have to follow your heart.

"Hi, Mr. Clark. You're back."

I smile wide and put my hand on the counter.

"Yes, Penny. I'm back."

Penny glances to the back of the store.

"Well, what can I do for you this time?"

I put my other hand up and look down at the gum.

"I didn't choose a gum when I was in before. Did I?"

"Is that what you want then? Gum?"

I look up from the gum and grin.

"They come out with a new flavour every day."

Penny leans forward and peers down.

"That's right. We got some Extreme Something or Other down there. Here."

Penny points to a bright pink package. I flip it up and slap it on the counter.

Penny smiles. Her eyebrows go up.

"Will that be all, Mr. Clark?"

I nod once deeply.

"How's the jaw harp? Can you play it?"

I tap my pocket.

"Got it right here, Penny. I'm gonna play it the first chance I get."

Penny laughs and I look back to the

pharmacist. He's busy and doesn't seem to know I'm here.

"Don't chew gum while you play."

That's when I notice. Penny has very pretty eyes. I couldn't see that before. Last time I was in town I couldn't see anyone's eyes.

"Sorry?"

"The gum. You don't wanna play and chew gum at the same time."

I feel concerned.

"Oh?"

"Yeah. You could fling your gum out at somebody. Turn your harp into a little sling shot."

I slip the harp out and open the box.

"That'll be one dollar and twenty-nine cents."

I fold the lid back on the box and shove it in my pants pocket this time, then fish a toonie out from under it.

Penny lets me drop the coin into her hand.

"Keep the change."

"No. No. You take your change."

I wave off the change and she gives a soft snort.

"In fact. You can keep the gum, too."

Penny cocks her head.

"Well, I think you're quite right about the harp. You keep the gum."

Penny watches my hand place the gum back on the counter.

"But . . ."

"No 'buts' about it, young lady. That gum is not going into this mouth and that's final."

"Okay. Well, here. Take your toonie back."

I raise a finger and wag it.

"Uh-uh. That's yours."

I let her figure it out.

"But you didn't buy anything."

I hear myself sigh.

"You don't think so?"

Penny slouches and laughs.

"I don't think you did, Mr. Clark."

"Well, let's just say you're keeping me from my business."

Penny looks worried.

"I'm just fooling around."

I take the toonie and drop it in my top pocket.

"Okay?"

Penny shrugs.

"Okay."

We look at each other for a while. I guess we're both trying to figure out whether we should just call it a day. I have kind of lost the moment a little so I just let us look at each other for a while then I turn and leave.

The police commotion is still going on at the Foodland. I walk along the sidewalk intending to go past.

"Mr. Clark! Mr. Clark!"

The store manager is calling my name. I stop and look. Two police officers who had been talking to the manager turn. I take a couple steps toward them and stop. I may be the person who did this but I'm not the *same* person. Some monumental shifts have taken place.

"What's going on **here?**"

The manager turns to a police officer.

"This is Mr. Clark, Officer. He owns the Sunoco at Cashtown. He's been here all morning. You been here all morning."

I move closer and bow slightly to the policemen. They just stare.

"Well, no. I just came in to drop off a lady's car, then I gotta head back to the pumps."

I smile and roll my eyes slightly. One of the policemen shifts his feet.

"You see anything strange, Mr. Clark? You see anybody in town this morning?"

I put my hand to my chin and look up squinting. I am aware that this looks a bit like I'm pretending to think, but it's all I could come up with. The other policeman turns to the manager.

"I think you better tell Mr. Clark what this is all about."

■ 4

One of the officers has said this to the manager. I am making a face now but it's impossible to know what it is. I can see their faces are starting to drift as well. Not full-on scribbles, but thumb-smudged. You can feel some of the easygoing quality of the day starting to go again. The two police officers stand at the side while the manager tells me all about this scene. Maybe it's a police technique. Get witnesses to talk to each other and just take notes. The manager's face is fat and smeared so I look at his hands. They are fat and red and moving as if he's breaking invisible sticks over and over again. The one hand leaves its companion for a moment and wipes down the front of his pants, then hangs forward. It doesn't grab the air right away but waits, watching the other hand, gauging its rhythms, then it goes up and matches perfectly. I am remembering this morning and some of the difficulty I had being in several places at once. They seemed to have categories for a while. One was thinking about the other. Then there were several different times at once. And another sort of spanned being different and managed to be very clearheaded. This makes me think that even though it's not possible to get things done properly in any one of these arrangements, it *is* possible to still be yourself, to still know you are here and, most importantly, to care about what happens. These hands are different though. They are clearly aware that the faces are blending downward a bit and that they will still talk to me. The hands will show me a way to stay here. Somebody *is* saying my name though. I feel like I've fallen through a trick mat into a pit on an island. You don't want to think about Mr. Howell and the Skipper and all of them, but something of Gilligan's problems are here right now. And the island supports this. It makes you think. It forces you to try to remember all the times he slapped you on the face and sprinkled coconut milk onto your lips, saying, "Wake up little buddy, wake up." I turn my face from side to side and watch the sky move. There is always something talking to us from somewhere else. It wants to quiet us. It wants us to know that sad is a frequency and that it picks it up like a radio signal. Then it pours a little room back in along the frequency, a little space around the things that have been touching for way too long. It touches every one of us.

So I am still here and probably looking up. The police are definitely taking an interest in me. And, like I said, I'm probably looking up and I hear them. It isn't anything powerful or tricky. I just listen.

"Mr. Clark? Are you driving?"

The manager's hands are either above me or below depending on whether you are looking up or down at me. I turn my face and I can feel that I am crying and smiling.

"He's having a bit of a shock, officer. Do you need a ride, Bob?"

Anyway, so one of the cops gives me a ride and I shoot him with his gun. That totally doesn't sound like it happened. That's very strange to me. Almost as if it's not quite enough to just say it at this particular time. I will try again to see. So. Well, there you go. I got this ride from a nice police officer because I didn't have one and, as it turns out, it was pretty easy to reach over and grab his gun and shoot it right at his head. So, anyway, he just dies like that. I got a ride form the cop and midway between Cashtown Corners and Creemore I put a bullet in his head. He's dead for sure. Like I said, I killed him pretty much just now and so things are going to get said again pretty soon. But for now let's just not act like we have to see it totally and let's just accept this report.

When he dies the cruiser goes for a while and I have to lean way down and pull his foot off the gas. I get out of the cruiser. It's not exactly pulled over. More parked in the oncoming lane so I have to move quickly. I put the vehicle in gear and slip over into the correct lane. The tiller's moving again and as I drive past, the gulls burrow backwards over the road. I slow the cruiser before I get to the station.

There's a black Tercel at number five. The hood's up and Jeremy is leaning against the grill. He must be putting in a can of oil. He turns away quickly when he sees the cruiser. I pull to the back beside the trailer and park it where the silver Corolla was.

In the rear view I see Jeremy fussing around the Tercel. He drops the hood, gives the cruiser a fast eyeball, then collects money from the driver. He steps back form the Tercel as it pulls away. Jeremy doesn't know it's me yet. He thinks a policeman has just pulled up and I would bet his mind is going at a pretty fair clip right about now. I make the conscious decision not to tell him everything right away.

Probably because he's turned into such an exciting person this morning and I don't want to ruin that. I also don't exactly know what I'm going to do now and explaining what I've done implies that I do and can only get confusing. So for now, I just get out of the cruiser and wave to him. It takes a few seconds for him to understand what he's looking at. He sees me standing here. I've just stepped out of the driver's side of a police cruiser and, that's right, Jeremy, I'm waving at you.

He doesn't wave back. He just stands there on the edge of the island. I stop waving. Jeremy steps off the island and I put up my hand.

"No, Jer. You watch the pumps. I'll be over in a minute."

Jeremy stops. He doesn't go back right away. He watches me go around to the passenger side. I have to yell.

"Jer! I'm serious! Just watch the pumps. Don't worry, I'll be over in a sec!"

Jeremy half turns, stops, completes the

turn and goes back to the island. I stand in the shadow of the canopy between number three and number four. He's going to watch, I guess. I scan the corners for cars. Jeremy does this too.

The dead cop droops to the ground from the passenger seat. I grab his belt and pull him out completely. I don't know how much of this Jeremy can see but I don't have time to worry about it. I pull up under the armpits and manage to hop him up my body. At the stairs I'm tempted to call Jeremy over for some help but he's gone back inside his booth. I can't see in the windows very well from here so I don't know if he's even watching.

I get the cop up the stairs and into the trailer. I'm very tired and out of breath so I only pull him in enough to close the door. I take his shoes off and put them on the lady's back. His jacket has a little blood on it but I clean it in the sink. I guess I need his shirt. His back is heavily haired with several intense-looking moles on his shoulders. I leave his pants and socks. The hat is a little big but if I angle it back a little it works. The holster is empty and I've left the gun in the car. I take one last look at myself and realize I'm being silly. There is not one good reason for me to be dressing up like a cop right now. I point at myself as if to say, "You know you're being goofy, don't you?" It's a nice crisp moment that tells me that some of the story I've been telling is going to settle again.

I make a stern face in the mirror. The cop hat falls forward and I tip it back with two fingers. It's the kind of thing you do before you call someone ma'am.

"Well, ma'am, looks like the problem is people. They just make us nervous and then we kill them. And then we feel better until somebody makes us nervous again. And, well, ma'am, that's the way it lays."

I'm a little amazed that I've managed to boil it down to something so simple. I don't make a very convincing cop though. I don't think there's much of a plan to work out there. No. I think the simple version is right. Stay away from people. Can't imagine going through life just killing anyone who made you feel nervous.

I step out into the sunshine and pop the cop sunglasses on. I can't find the gun right away, then fishing around, it's there, under the seat. Jeremy is standing at the door watching me walk across the lot. He steps away from the glass as I hop up onto the island. I catch a glimpse of my reflection before I pull the door open.

Jeremy has scurried around behind the cash register.

"I thought you were a cop."

I take off the hat.

"Ta-da! Just me."

I look at Jeremy to see what he thinks. He looks like he was going to try to play it off as funny but then his face falls a little bit. I keep forgetting that Jeremy is not me.

"Sorry. Couldn't resist."

Jeremy leans to the side and looks out at the cruiser.

"What's going on?"

In a funny flash it occurs to me that Jeremy could easily have called the police so this must be just making him feel crazy right now.

"Did you think you'd called the police or something?"

Jeremy looks startled.

"Okay. Well, I'm just going to tell you where we're at and then let you do whatever you want."

Jeremy doesn't look particularly relieved.

"Oh, and the money is still yours too."

Jeremy has no expression.

"So. Well. I've been killing people today. First I killed her. That one. You know. Then I killed Mrs. _____ at the Foodland. Then I killed a policeman. That's three people. What about that, huh?"

Jeremy. Jeremy. Jeremy.

"So I can tell you how each one happened but I don't think that's really gonna matter much in the end."

I pull out the gun. Not sure why but Jeremy just about faints.

"So, it looks like I have a condition of some kind where I have to kill people in order to get myself back on track or something. So I've decided to just disappear."

Jeremy looks up from the gun.

"What? Say it? I can see you wanna ask."

Jeremy looks like his mouth's a little dry. But he manages a word.

"What?"

"Disappear. Stay away from people. Get out of all youses hairs for good."

Jeremy nods to this.

"I can't kill myself. So that's that."

I put the gun back in the holster.

"Bye, Jer."

He doesn't say anything and it's a bit awkward so I just adjust my hat and leave.

I step out between pump two and pump

three and stroll across the lot. I feel him looking and I stop. He's watching me alright. Got his hand up shielding his eyes and his nose to the glass.

"Bye, Jer," I say but he can't hear me. I do the little ma'am two-finger salute off the brim and turn away. Not walking quite yet though. I stand in the parking lot. I'm twenty-five feet or so away from the door. I have started to leave but I still don't have anywhere to go. The gulls are up high in the air. The trailer obscures my view of the field so I don't know if the tiller's moving or not. I put my hands on my hips and sigh. I'm glad I have my own socks and underwear on still. The sun feels good on my shoulders.

Ding. Ding.

A car. A blue minivan has pulled up to two and three. I almost run but stop myself. Take a breath. There's a cruiser right there and a cop right over here. All we are is something that he's looking at from his minivan. I almost give him the two-finger but stop myself. Then I notice Jeremy. He's walking up the shoulder of the highway. He's halfway up the hill on his way to Avening. Where the hell is he going? I walk toward the minivan and the man rolls down his window.

"Hello, officer."

I hook my hand on the top of the window but don't take my eyes off Jeremy.

"Well, sir. There he goes."

The man cranes around in his seat to look.

"Who?"

"That'd be the guy who's supposed to pump your gas."

We watch Jeremy reach the top of the hill then step down the other side and out of sight. The man turns back to me.

"There's nobody pumping gas?"

I smile and look back to the top of the hill. The man waits patiently while I stare at the road. In time I lean back down hooking both hands over the glass.

"Doesn't look that way. Doesn't look that way at all."

The man looks over at the cruiser parked beside the trailer. He looks like he has a question he wants to ask.

"Well, officer, I guess we'll just head up the road and hope . . ." He doesn't finish the sentence. He lets his hands explain it away by gesturing out toward the highway.

I straighten up and slap the side of his minivan. He goes to put it in gear but I get an idea.

"Hey, hang on a sec. You need gas?"

The man doesn't answer. He looks in the back of the van and I can make out two children sitting in booster seats.

"Let me see what I can do."

I stroll around the back of the van. The cruiser sits there beside the trailer and I'm pretty sure it doesn't look quite right. I'm aware I'm grafting this part of my story to another that isn't obvious anymore.

I flip open his gas door and drop the nozzle in. The minivan windows—all of them—come down.

"Officer? Hello?"

I see my sunglasses and hat reflected in the tinted glass.

"You'll have to turn your engine off, sir."

I hear a little girl's voice.

"I smell gas, Daddy. Can you put my window up?"

I step back up onto the island and select his grade. The car engine stops and the windows go back up. The hose pulses to life against my knee. If nothing else I've bought some time to figure out what's next. Take stock. I'm going to have to walk somewhere from here. Into the booth. Back to the cruiser. Into the trailer. But then where? I have to not be anymore. Thirty-five litres. I feel the gas getting near the top. Do I die? The trigger releases. Not going to die. You can't decide to die just because of pressure. Fifty-seven dollars and thirty-six cents. Forty. Fifty. Sixty. Release. Got to ease off a bit. Seventy. Eighty. Back off. Ninety. Five. Six. Seven. Eight. Nine. And fifty-eight dollars zero. I squeeze one last time at the six and ease off till the end.

I come around the back of the van again. The driver's window starts to come down.

"There you go. Full up."

The man looks nervous.

"Okay. Great. How much do I owe you?"

I stretch and straighten up.

"Oh. You don't owe me anything. He's . . . uh . . . the guy's not here. So don't worry about it."

"I'd like to pay, officer. Can I leave it with you? How much was it?"

He turns back to read the pump.

"Here, I'll give ya sixty. Does that cover it? Don't worry about the change."

I look at the three twenties.

"No, sir. I can't take that. Against regulations."

"Okay. Can you put it inside or I can . . ."

"You have a nice trip. Drive safe. And watch the speed."

I rap the roof with my knuckles and step

back. The man slumps a little and looks forward. He's chewing his mouth up as he curls the bills into his shirt pocket. The van starts but sits for a moment. The man turns and looks at me, then over to the cruiser. Hand to the wheel and into gear. He gives me an abrupt accepting nod and rolls the van toward the road. I stay still for a moment. No waving. I realize that it makes me anxious to separate fully from them but it doesn't seem right to make too much out of it. I turn and walk back toward the trailer. The van sits at the edge of the road and I can't tell if he's watching me so I try to walk as if I've already forgotten about them and have moved on. I reach the back of the cruiser but I've already made up my mind that I'm going to leave it here. The van hasn't moved so he may still be watching. I can't step up into the trailer so I get into the cruiser.

There's blood on the window and the steering wheel is sticky. I don't want to sit in here. The van is gone so I remove the hat and start unbuttoning the shirt. There is blood

moving through this cruiser like spiders
jumping.

■ 5

I am standing at precisely the centre point of Cashtown Corners. Right at the point where two centre lines intersect. There are not many places on earth as simple and perfect as this. Every single square inch has the same influence on me and I am completely impartial. I am going to move from this spot and I think there has to be a reason. I could wait for a car and then step off the road and walk in the direction it came from. Or the direction it goes. I could close my eyes and turn in circles. Count to a number and stop. The number should matter. Fifty-seven. I could sing one of those children's songs that determines who will be "it." I face north. The road ascends high toward a Jeffrey Deere warehouse. Then

a butcher's. A greenhouse. Then Stayner. Stay.
I turn and face south. The road climbs and
then curves and rolls. Fields and farms and
eventually Avening. The speed limit barely
changes through Avening. Evening. I turn and
face west. A level line past the worm-heavy
birds. Creemore. The Mad and Noisy River.
More. This is a stupid anthem or something.
A car appears from Creemore and I go east.
Sirens. I go southeast into a cornfield.

The corn swallows me whole and I move
quite quickly between the rows. The ears of
corn batter my head and, above, the siren
screams in the sky like a wheeling bird. I
slip along the limitless stalks with my hands
pressed on either side of my nose. I run with my
eyes shut, letting the weight of the ears centre
me. I will run and run and run. The sirens are
multiplying but they sound farther away. I run
and run and run. I feel silk gathering on my
hands and in my hair like a mask. It traps my
breath so that hot puffs beat my face. The silk
hairs are massing on my shoulders and back,

slowing me. I start to stomp as I grow clumsy with the weight. I stop. I am under a cloak of dense white beards. Slipping my hands down without disturbing the cover I lower myself and sit cross-legged in the dirt. The sirens aren't as tall anymore. They can still be heard cutting and falling, but far away. My own sound is louder. My breathing. My full nose. I have become a bull now, with a towering back and wet buried eyes and a loud heavy face. I will not move. Breathing. Breathing. Breathing.

I don't know exactly where I am. If I ran a mile or less. Or more. I don't know if I am visible from anywhere. If I will be caught soon. I sit in this hot dark effigy, waiting. They could be here now. Surrounding this. Trying to understand what they have here before moving in on it. Guns drawn. A finger to a lip and hand gesturing "Move up, move up," then: "Wait." The hand turns. The sirens stop. The sirens have stopped. The sirens stop because they've all arrived. The sirens announce the coming and the silence marks the arrival. The lot at the gas bar must be full of cruisers. Officers jump out and, drawing weapons, split into two groups. One encircles the booth. The other forms flanks around the trailer. Do they move in on both at once? The booth is empty. The map might still be down, leaning against the wall under the safe. In the trailer they make the big discovery. The dead officer and a face-down Jane Doe. A deep spasm will go through the area. Everything and everyone will soon be deployed. I hear a scratching. Some small animal. What animals live in a cornfield? Mice? Groundhogs? The scratching stops. A wind moves at a distance; it seems to circle quickly, then brush over me. I think I have to accept that nothing might happen to me for a good long while. The heat is held in by the silk and long prickly lines are running down my back and arms. The daylight can't get in so I don't know if the sun is on me or if the corn shades me.

I mark time by listening to myself. I have

had a terrible series of shocks today. Yes, the things that happened were things that I did. And if I am ever caught and have to stand up in front of you, you'll wonder what goes on in a person like me. That's what I'm listening for now. I am aware that anything I might say I would have to invent. I would say what I think a person like me would say. But for now, I'm just listening. I want to know precisely what I am. And that is what I am right now. Listening silently to myself listening silently. And I agree, it sounds an awful lot like there is nothing to hear but that puts me beside you. We're both very quiet now. We're both just here. I accept this. God, it didn't start this way though, did it?

■ 6

I was wrong. The sunlight was reaching me. Now it is night. And black and still hot. The ground beneath has soaked up so much of my sweat that I sit in mud. Something came close and sniffed at me. A raccoon? A possum? It gave a warning snarl and then drifted off. I hear a crackling noise over me. Bats, I think. It may be time to crawl out from behind here. I am about to do this, to slip out from under this husk of me, when a new sound, a very big sound, batters down from above. It's the heavy flapping noise of a helicopter. And then a brilliance seizes my face. It moves off, pulling darkness back, then rolls to my right and goes. The helicopter blades seem to change velocity a little, then roar back to full thunder. They are above me. Searching. The white punches against me again and the rattle shakes the dry paste in my ears. I wait to be kicked. To be shot. To be suspended in midair and examined. I wait for a long glowing appendage to pierce my face and pull me up in a single violent suck. There is no way to know. There is no way to know. And then it goes away.

■ 7

The morning comes and I haven't moved. I guess that it's about noon when I hear a single siren. It's hard to say where it comes from or where it goes to. It sounds like it comes from there and goes to about there. Nothing happens today. I almost throw up late in the afternoon and am not sure that I'm fully conscious for this. Just before dusk a flock of geese flies low overhead. Their honking is so horrible and raw that I shit through my pants into the ground. I think there must be a moon because I watch a short silver line move slowly down my shin throughout the night. No animals come to me. No helicopters shine on me.

■ 8

It is difficult to turn my head. The silk and dust have turned to heavy clay and hardened to me. I am breaking out of a statue now. I push my jaw forward and feel the shell pull off of my ears. I hunch my shoulders and this separates the top section from the bottom. I brace for hard light but it's not; the corn is still green and it cools and calms the air around me. It turns out that I am deep beneath a waving roof of plants. If I am to take any cues from these first moments then I still have something left to do. I am still moving. I leave the broken bust behind and begin to lope, slouching as much away as toward and decide that I will do massive, decisive things when I get there.

There is the sudden end of corn stalks. I

step out of them like a ghost from a cage and instantly feel the weight of my shadow fall in the short grass beside me. The grass gets sparer up ahead, the bare bright earth then a yard. I blink at the house to try to make it appear clearer. Orange brick. A small white porch with thick wooden posts. Two-storey. Something tugs the back of my pants down and in pulling them up I find that I still have the policeman's gun. Guns seem to know when you might use them and they will draw down a little heavier in anticipation. So I point the gun at the house.

I don't bother knocking and enter the house through a side door. This leads directly into an office. A heavy wooden desk. Cabinets. Book shelves. There are degrees on the wall. Business degrees. Accounting. The floor snaps when I stop moving so I keep walking out into a larger room. A washing machine and an unfinished basement full of cardboard boxes. A plywood reindeer. Diffuse sunlight hangs out from a sunken window. From high above there is movement. Quick steps down stairs. Someone saw me. Someone knows I'm here and they're running to the phone. The footsteps come from directly above me. Calmer now. They stop. A kettle is whistling. I hadn't noticed that. The whistle whines low **and** stops. There are stairs leading up to this floor. What must be the kitchen. I take them. Not fast and not slow, but deliberately enough and through the door. It is a kitchen. A woman in a bathrobe leans against a counter, looking out the window and eating toast. A cup of steeping tea steams on a table. She turns and I catch a flash of the satin red beneath the robe and fire. She flops forward, bouncing her head up and off the table before slipping to the ground. She dies. The toast turns in her mouth, then rides in blood across the floor. I fire again at the wall. Twice. I don't know why. In the quiet that follows I hear other feet move overhead.

The third floor is clearly a separate apartment because I open the door on a second, smaller kitchen. This woman is older. She is giant. The mother of the other woman. She holds an empty plate waiting for toast to pop. She turns to me. Her voice is completely unexpected.

"Who are you?"

She drops the plate and tries to run past me but I push her by the neck to the wall and shoot a hole in her just above the left eye. She drops straight down and I shoot again. I empty the gun into the wall. The toast pops and makes me jump. I throw the gun into the sink. This woman was so large that her knees have snapped under her weight. Without muscle and the will to support herself, her meagre pillars broke. I take a towel from a hamper sitting under the table and curl it on the floor around her head. I'm not cleaning up, can't see the point, but I'm keeping surfaces safe for me to run over.

In the downstairs kitchen the younger woman has bled a shiny dark pool across the floor and under the stove. I decide I'm going to keep people together. Put them somewhere. I don't question myself about this. I just assume keeping any order right now is better than the alternative. I hold her ankles and drag her, looking aside when the red satin falls above her thighs. Through a short hall and into an expansive sitting room. Too big for a sitting room. Almost a ballroom with high ornate windows and columns and a single pink settee with thick scrolled arms. I lay her in the middle of the floor and return to the kitchen. I realize I am walking along a red road that tracks about forty feet through the house from her head in the ballroom to the broken tea cup in the kitchen. I scoop three kitchen towels from the oven door and walk the blood path back to her body. I consider cleaning the floor but that would only be moving blood out farther and farther through the house. I drop the towels on her face. I walk back out into the hall looking for a room I have not seen yet. The master bedroom. The bed is crisply made and the drapes are drawn. The effect here is of a time capsule. A place left for future generations to discover. A framed picture of the astronauts from Apollo 13 hangs above a bureau. Nineteen sixty-eight, at least. But it feels more like the fifties. I pull the sheets out from the corner of the bed and wipe blood from my hands. I have to turn and twist the fabric to drag thickening red strands from under my nails. I release the sheets and they stick out from the bed's perfect surface like fingers ripping at the back edge of a sea. There is a door leading off from the back of this room. A bathroom with a shower. I look at myself quickly. My face is still patched with yellow wafers and fibres. Fine blood speckles cover my eyelids and forehead. I turn the shower on and adjust it to near scalding. My clothes come off me and stand like sticks. I lift them and drop them in the toilet where water quickly wicks up and pulls the fabric down.

The shower removes everything in seconds. Blood and mud and sweat and shit coils down my legs and makes heavy brown river deltas off my toes to the drain. My shoulders move independently for the first time. My chest heaves out and drops. I cannot change, This is not the time to change. The shower is a dangerous place. The wrong thing to do. If I change, if I reach a different idea about what is happening, then I will be destroyed. I punch the shower off and step out through steam into the bathroom.

There are suits in a closet. I pull one out and toss it on the bed. I snap open other drawers and find socks and underwear and an undershirt. And a gun. A very old looking handgun. It is clean and loaded and I lay it on the bed beside my new clothes.

I have noticed but not mentioned that there are family photos all through the house. There are people yet who will be coming home for dinner and I have to get ready for them.

■ 9

I try to pull the large woman by the legs. I want her downstairs, too. Make it easy for God to collect them if they're all in one room. Her legs are clearly snapped in half at the knee and when I try to pull her massive weight they thin to the point of almost popping off completely. I try pulling the carpet she lies on; she's too heavy and I give up. Something about her just lying there bothers me. Her immensity. The sheer volume of flesh twisted and hanging from her bare legs. I take a stack of newspapers and spread them over her. I notice a clock hanging on the side of the cupboard. The only one I've seen in the entire house. It's noon and I suddenly feel hungry.

The fridge is full of rolled-up paper bags

and preserves. I avoid these and find a chunk of pork shoulder wrapped in cellophane. I make a sandwich and pour myself a glass of milk. There's a bird feeder visible through the kitchen window. As I eat I watch the finches being bullied by grackles. The grackles wait until three or four finches settle and peck then they swoop in. Once the finches have flown to a nearby apple tree, the grackles head back over a stone wall and wait to do it again. This must be what Helen was watching while she ate her toast. I rinse my dishes in the sink and stand them in the drying rack. There's a rake leaning against the stone wall and the ground along its edge has been pulled clean. A pile of bramble and leaves sits off the end by the spindle of a clothes-drying rack. There are six or seven pairs of black socks pegged to the lines.

I am outside. The bramble still holds tight in the corner where the wall meets the house and I drive the rake back against the stone and pull forward. This only draws the top layer off, which I kick free. The rest holds tough and I have to choke up on the rake to get any deeper. It's frustrating work. The dense tangle of vegetation resists and holds tight to the ground. It feels good on my arms though, and I feel the food I ate quickly metabolizing into energy in my muscles. The pile near the clothes grows and eventually I have cleared the last section of the wall. I look around for where it might have been destined. In the distance on a small embankment I see three mounds of compost. The first mound is new, some green, some crunchier looking, all dead. The second pile is leaves decomposing into a fine deep brown strata. The third and final stage is black, almost delicious looking. Just behind the end of the wall there is wheelbarrow heavily caked with old concrete. I fill this about a dozen times, bouncing across the yard to the first compost mound. When the transfer is complete I clean the trail of debris with the rake. I have bent three tines up on one side. I have pushed harder on it than the previous user. Probably Helen. Probably not the husband. I wonder if he's gone. Dead or left. I pull the socks from the line as I walk back to the house. The pegs pop off as I do this, scaring grackles from the wall. I collect the pegs scattered in the dirt and feed them into a cloth bag that hangs midway up the spindle. The grackles make mechanical squeaking noises at me as I slide open the screen to the kitchen. I have trouble drawing it closed as it catches in the rut. I hear a low gasp, a sigh from somewhere. It sounds like air brakes on a truck. Or a bus. A school bus.

■ 10

I had almost forgotten. I had gotten used to
something else and I wasn't thinking. This is
not good. Not good. My stomach is pitching
around like a cat in a bag. I have to kill children
now. It suddenly doesn't seem real. It can't be
possible. I can't. I run through to the back of
the house along the dry blood road and reach
the master bedroom. The corner of the bed.
The gun sits beside the tie I didn't put on. I
pick up the gun and spin into the bathroom.
My chest drops down hard across my middle
and I throw up in the sink. Chewed pork
shoulder makes a pink splatter pattern. My
throat bucks back once, then hoses the sink
with white-pink liquid. I look up. A capillary
has blown in my right eye and it shines at me

with shark-like robotic opacity. I blink once over the hard crimson ball.

Which door will they come to? I don't want to see them. I want to shoot them in darkness. From somewhere I can't see them. I stand in the archway leading out of the ballroom to the hallway. I hear keys and run to the centre front door. I stand flat against the wall so that when the door opens I am behind it. Unseen. Unseeing. The door pulls in. It doesn't open inward. I am exposed here. I am not behind anything when the girl backs in and drops a knapsack on the rug. She has her back to me. I just don't want to be seen. I don't want to hear her. I raise the gun when I sense she will turn and I fire into the back of her head. She drops but is stopped and sent forward when her hips lock on the way down. I reach out and grab her hair, pulling back to prevent her from falling out the open door. Her body rests curved back toward the hall. I kick the knapsack halfway up the hall and drag her by the ankles. I am

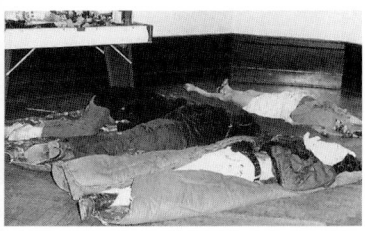
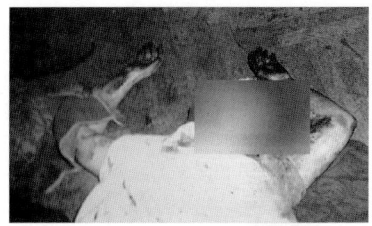

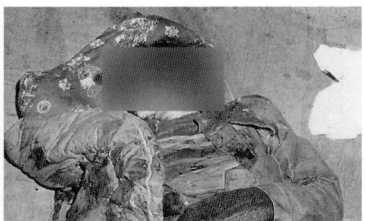
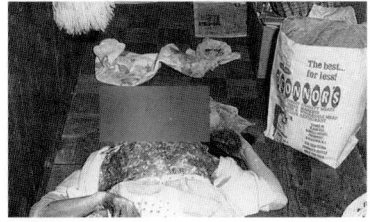

Bodies laid out on sleeping bags by Bob Clark in the "ballroom." The bodies (top right going clockwise) of Jeffrey Jr., Alma Faruzi, and Patty Lerner. These photos were found on Helen Lerner's camera. The faces of the victims are extremely distressing, and have been blurred at the family's request.

The real Jeffrey Lerner with Helen in happier times. Lerner, a deeply religious man, left his family and moved, without telling them where he was going, to a trailer park in Denver, Colorado. He claimed his family had "abandoned God" and has remained silent about the slayings.

Helen Lerner worked at a vinegar factory to support her family.

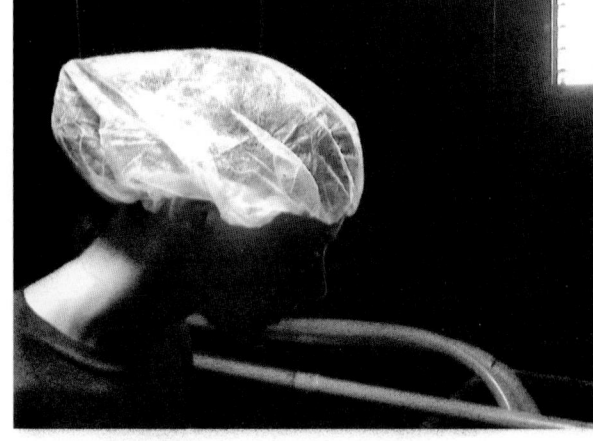

"I think there's more than one," pump jockey Jeffrey _____ answered ominously when asked by police about his boss, Bob Clark.

The gas station at Cashtown Corners owned and operated by Bob Clark. The bodies of Miriam Holly and Constable McCormack were discovered on this property.

Decorative scarecrows are popular in the region. On at least three occasions, police fired their weapons into these often life-like figures while searching the cornfields.

The Lerner home became Bob Clark's slaughterhouse and hideout. Clearview Township is so named because of its bucolic panoramas. Clark was, ironically, hiding in plain view—the Lerner House was visible for miles and could, in fact, be seen clearly from the intersection where the killing began.

MR.
BAKER
STAFF

1022
4

Charlie Baker is an art teacher, rugby coach, and musician at Duntroon Secondary School.

Patty Lerner was one of his favourite students. A talented visual artist whose work appeared in numerous student shows.

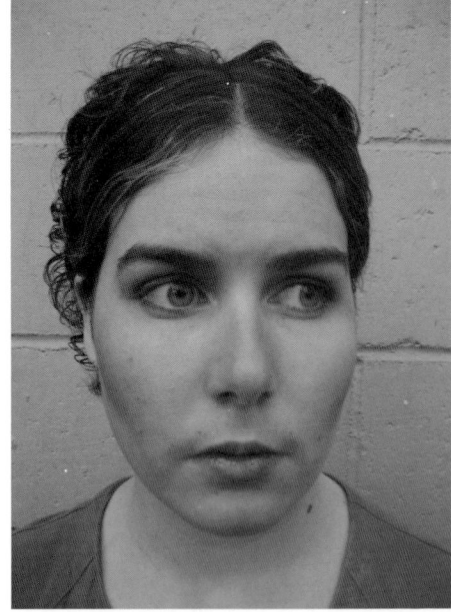

This sculpture was created by Patty Lerner in Charlie Baker's grade 12 art class. The World Trade Center Birdhouse was, according to Baker, her "moving tribute" to the events of September 11, 2001. She created her tribute to those who died one month before she would lose her own life to a madman.

Charlie Baker remains a popular teacher. He had several bizarre encounters with Bob Clark who pretended to be Jeffrey Lerner while living, sleeping, and eating in the Lerner home.

The Duntroon Secondary School Yearbook, which came out after the murders, contained numerous moving homages produced by Charlie Baker's art class. Depicted here is an image of Patty Lerner. Charlie himself set the example: life must go on.

Patty Lerner, top left, in a dramatic production mounted by the Duntroon Secondary School Drama Club.

Left: The Lerner House. A haunted shell that still sends shivers through Clearview Township.

Below: The "vintage" pickup truck that Bob Clark claimed to have won through a local raffle. Local officials were quick to set the record straight when national media erroneously repeated Clark's claim.

Above: One of the weapons used by Bob Clark to destroy an innocent family. Like many things the police discovered that day, it had the appearance of a prop in a tragic stage production.

Below: The Lerner ballroom.

WOLFGANG AMADEUS MOZART

Left: When police moved in to arrest Clark, he was blasting Mozart's "Requiem" at ear-splitting volumes. One officer on the scene later described it as the strangest setting for an arrest he'd ever experienced, claiming that "it felt like an actual nightmare. It even had its own soundtrack!"

Below: This photograph was taken by Sophy Pollack, a classmate of Patty Lerner, in the late autumn following the killings. Sophy claims, and many believe her, that Patty can be seen in the picture turning toward the camera. The Lerner house has not been occupied since the murders and is now firmly established as a haunted structure according to local lore.

In the year following the murders, Charlie Baker tasked his class with making copies of Patty's tribute to 9/11 for a section of his course covering multiples in sculpture. He said they were tributes to a tribute.

in a hurry to get her into a sleeping bag. I do not want to see her face. She leaves a thinner lighter line of red that comes out the front, not the back, of her head. I plant her beside a bag next to her mother and I roll her onto her back. Her face flips up to the ceiling and it's not as bad as I thought. The bullet exited between her eyebrows and burst open the bottom half of her forehead. Her face is fine. Her eyes are half closed. Drowsy looking. I zip her in quickly and become aware that I have been speaking rapidly to myself. About what, I don't know. Then I stand and actually pump my arms up over my head and yell.

Yeah! Yeah! Yeah! Yeah! Yeah!

"Hello? You left a door open!"

Another one. That's fine. It's better if this all happens fast. Where's my gun? I slip in the fresh blood as I turn into the hall and have to push on a pillar to not fall. The gun is on the floor by the knapsack. I scoop it up and see the boy. He's on one knee untying a shoe. He's a big kid. The older. The bullet drives through the side of his head, pushing it into the closed door. He dies pulling his laces to either side of his shoe. I fire the gun back up the hallway as if there were someone coming from the kitchen. I fire four times, emptying the gun. Noise downstairs. Someone is downstairs. I drop the gun to the floor and step briskly but as silent as I can to the stairs leading to the basement. The youngest. I descend the stairs without a gun. A short wall stops me from being seen. I look frantically for a weapon. It seems that I am afraid that the young boy will kill me if he sees me. There is nothing here. A laundry basket. A jug of detergent. I try to picture beating someone with it. I even test its weight with my toe. No good. I step out into the open and he's there. Back to me, putting a backpack on a hook. I move forward. scanning the floor from edge to edge. A small sack of washers. Three bags of fertilizer. A short bat. Thin. A kid's bat, but wooden at least. I lift it and it feels too light, but I have no time left.

I swing and it bounces. Again. Swing and bounce. Swing and bounce. I'm just going to have to keep doing this without saying it every time.

■ 11

The moon is halved by darkness. Its silver falls as gold onto corn seas. The seas are calm and carried through the night on long swells. No ships. No land. Nothing under the sky but infinite yellow vegetation in shining sleeves. Where the sun has caught the moon there are no stars but against its invisible profile furious sets of foam turn and spill. A torn cloud grows sideways along the moon's eye. A fine oil is scattered out from the white crawlspace of a half galaxy. The oil is orange and green and gold that sprays behind the moon and emerges toward the unseen sun as a brief map. Black scratched lines that hold for a second then scatter as a million tiny viruses vibrating on the scalp of a whale. Foxes turn their teeth into the ground and slice through the faces of grubs. The insides of headless worms drift up and make cold wet rings around the tiny holes where they had been. People in Creemore have died. Slaughtered. A bomb has gone off in the Foodland and quartered people slam against its beams. The silver path down to the river from Avening is clogged with bleating pigs that can gain no footing in their neighbours' slippery livers. In New Lowell people drink rare cancer and it flows down their cheeks into the dishes of dogs anxious to die. And here in my new house in the corn with my nostrils and lungs frosted red from such deep blood breathing, I drop a stylus into a lizard black pool of vinyl. The speakers hammer to life. Not just the ones here beside me, but from speakers hidden throughout the house, assaulting every cube of air. The voices surge and fall as complete oceans. Despairing and terrible oceans. Entire choirs meet across deep trenches, pitched across time-angry distances into each other. The Bible marches slowly through the house. Its crashing boots throw salt water up the windows. Its tiny armadillo face pokes out from between mountain arms. Religious music. I check. Mozart's Requiem. I look back over the dead five. We have set a trap for God.

The voices soften as I reach the bottom of the stairs. Not human. Each bevelled pipe selects a child and enters his back to blow through bones. Mothers' screams chase past me as I ascend. The kitchen light. Eyes. I open the fridge. Beards. The fridge light. Teeth. The bathroom light. Fingers. The hall light. Shoulders. The bedroom light. Throats and shoulders. Back down stairs over bent spines and open ribs. The hall light. The kitchen. The bathroom. The master bedroom. Another bedroom. Another. Another.

The windows are being pulled inward by a choir that has just drawn its final breath and the glass bows outward driven by the force of my ten thousand lights. I step past the bodies on the beach and lower myself on the pink settee. I face the large window and can see myself again.

And now I wait to see who I can catch first: God or the rest of you.

■ 12

It is morning and I am asleep. In my dream a grackle is pecking rhythmically on the crown on my head. Tchsk. Tchsk. Tchsk. Tchsk. I wake and straighten my head. My neck has pulled painfully tight by sleeping in this position. I blink my eyes open. The sun is just above the window top but the light is powerful enough to hurt my eyes. The grackle is still etching away. I turn to the record player and see the stylus snipping back and forth at the end of the album. I rise slowly, stiffly. Without bothering to lift the arm I just shut the entire system down by depressing a silver dome with two fingers. Silence. The floor is cold on my bare feet as I take a wide path around the bodies in sleeping bags. I am thankful now that I had done this. It's too early to be looking at dead people's faces.

In the kitchen I find some bread in the freezer and push the hard slices into the toaster. There are no birds at the feeder. I let my mind wander a little but am cautious. It was her. That woman who wouldn't obey the green. I try to remember what I thought about what I had done back then. I can't recall. It seemed I had made smallish explanations. And now, no matter what I thought I had done or why I did it, it has become completely untrue because of what I have done since. The toast snaps up and I stop thinking. It is hot in my fingers and the cold butter I push across it liquefies. It is splendid to eat. I devour the first slice in three bites then carry the second back into the hall. I am better this morning and consider bringing this all to an end. It's clear to me that the father isn't part of the picture. And for some reason the police haven't bothered to look beyond their immediate surroundings. I am the one who has to act. To bring it to a close.

The idea of dying occurs again. I can't seem to get a picture of how this would happen. I have no gun anymore and even if I did, I can't imagine deliberately pulling the trigger and setting into motion events that end in my brains getting pushed out. I could hang. There are railings and beams in here. Trees and roof edges out there. But then I come to the same moment. The decision to step into air and be suspended by my neck. It's the decision. The simple stepping off. The light squeeze of a finger. It appalls me and makes me shiver. I am calmed by the idea of not being here but I cannot stomach the mechanism that takes me away. I will not die.

There are two phones in this house as far as I can tell. A wall phone in the kitchen and a phone on a black stool before the archway into the ballroom. Probably one that I didn't see in the office downstairs. And possibly in the apartment upstairs. Telephones. Old ones with cords and cold plastic shapes. I lift the one in the archway. It has buttons, so it's probably from the seventies. I could just call the police and tell them where I am. I wouldn't have to say it twice, that's for sure. *Officer, if you look up the road you can probably see the house from where you stand.* He might have to step outside to see it. There would be a vast eruption of sirens again, from every corner of the globe it would feel like. Tactical teams in storm trooper getups. Plastic shields and battering teams of two. Snipers maybe, might come in first and position themselves in trees. A perimeter, it's called. A perimeter would have to be established. And at the base of the driveway, a dozen cruisers parked in the tall grass along the shoulder. They could get me easy. I could leave it to them to shoot me. Come spinning out the front door and just take rounds until I cartwheeled off the front porch. I would be gone then. Or I could come out slowly and offer my hands to them. Be led away past rows of cops lowering their assault weapons, like bridesmaids letting flowers drift from their hands. The groom is led away past the denied party. The bride lies slain at the preacher's feet. I would never speak after that. No matter what they asked. No matter what. I would sit for the rest of my life on whatever chair they put under me and I would never utter a word. Ever. For decades. Ever. I like this idea. It's like placing myself in a cocoon that no one can see. I eat in there and when I move to lie down I sleep in there. I decide that I don't have to wait until they find me to do this. I can start now. I am impatient. I am starting now. I return to the settee and sit. This is the last you will ever see or hear of me.

■ 13

Before you start laughing at me, please hear me out. I really was never coming back. I really did sit in an invisible cocoon on the settee. I said nothing and I didn't move. Okay, I got up twice to go to the bathroom. And I heated up a can of soup. But I was there for *hours*. How many do you think? Five? Six? Think of sitting in the same spot for six hours. I did. For *sixteen hours*. The night descended and there was a thunderstorm. By morning the house was beginning to smell. And I stayed sitting well into the afternoon. Until now. Why did I not stay in the cocoon forever? I can't say exactly, but at some point, bit by bit, it became obvious that no one could do it. In spite of my deep and abiding commitment, a commitment that brought me to the brink of it, I could not do this impossible thing. I was crying at one point and I wanted to say so. But I didn't. The telephone rang and I almost answered it but I didn't. Still, a point came, call it the curvature of the earth, call it an itch on my face, call it what you will, but the point came when I was forced to move and given no choice. Only those of us who have sat at the edge of eternity know the name of the force that shoves you back.

I figured out it was Sunday today and that's why the school hasn't called. At least, that's not who called earlier. It is Sunday though and these people would have gone to church this morning. I decide that if the pastor comes to the door I will give myself up to him. I have also wondered, while sitting on that foul couch for a week, where are the damn police? Where are they in their investigation? I am craving something. Anything.

I find the television set under a brown cloth at the back of a closet off the hallway. I drag it into the ballroom, leaving black lines on the floor and white lines in the blood. I'm relieved to find that, though ancient, the TV is not black and white. There is no cable or satellite so I have to flip a hooped antenna up and down to find a station. I manage to get an unsteady but watchable feed of the A channel out of Barrie. I have shoved the settee down the stairs and shattered it. It was a source of embarrassment. So I sit on the floor. Where I sit affects the reception and I wind up far to the right of the screen. I inch myself back and closer to the middle with imperceptible little hops I manage by pushing down with my palms. I stop periodically and wait to see if the television has noticed then move again.

The smell seems less dense down here. If I stand or, worse, if I walk around stirring the air, a poisonous finger gags me with its sick tip and I almost vomit. I have not eaten since the soup and feel no desire to put food in my mouth. I watch an episode of *Law & Order* that I have seen twice before. It's based on a real news story about a group of terrorists foiled in the streets of Manhattan, but veers suddenly into a plot by a jealous stepmother to have her daughter killed. Nothing in this episode causes me to reflect on my own situation. Theme music with brassy horns. News. A ticker line scrolls across the bottom before an image appears.

POLICE SAY PUMP JOCKEY COP KILLER

It rolls past once and repeats. It's Jeremy. Jeremy, he's being led from a van and takes two steps and disappears into a building. There is a scrum, a crush of people, press and photographers. A large policeman steps in front and several others join him. They stand in a grim wall.

The anchor appears. A thin woman standing in a way that makes her look stressed. She holds pages down against a black skirt.

"Police say that since detaining Jeremy _____, the pump jockey found walking away from the scene of Friday's horrific police slaying at Cashtown Corners, they are getting no co-operation from their suspect. In spite of the fact that he was picked up with twelve thousand dollars cash determined later to have been taken from the gas station safe, police have yet to lay charges and continue interrogating the suspect, prompting his appointed council to request that either their client be charged or released. As well as the slain officer, two other victims were discovered on Friday, one at the scene and another in the Nearby Village of Creemore. The owner of the gas station has not been seen since Friday and police believe he may be a fourth victim."

And there I am. From a picture taken of me and Don Cherry seven years ago when he stopped for gas. They've cut Don from the picture and blown up my face. I rock forward onto my knees and the reception dissolves. I slap both hands down flat.

I turn to the room behind me.

"That was me! That was me!"

I stand and start pacing. They have Jeremy. They think he did it. But how could they? The woman in Creemore. They saw me there. How can they think he did that? And that man with his kids in the van, I talked to him dressed as a cop. Surely he recognized me in the photo? Unless he really didn't. And he thought I really was a cop. He thinks I was *the* cop. I want to know. I want to know. I am pacing quickly in circles and don't see the sleeping bag until my foot hooks under it. I fall flat across three bags and force horrible gases to bellow out. I roll off to the side and cannot breathe. Vomit is slapping the floor all around me as I stand. I collapse against the television and it falls forward and implodes. I seal my mouth with two hands and head downstairs.

I will be bruised. I sit at the desk and try to think. This is important information. This changes everything. Am I free now? Can this possibly mean that I can just walk away? I'll never do anything like this again, that goes without saying, but can it be true? There are slippery holes in it. Trip wires all over it. I don't think it's safe or lasting. It's a window though. It's an opportunity. It occurs to me that something, some power greater than me, wants me to get away. I have confessed. And now that I have, almost by accident, passed through these heavy challenges, I have emerged a changed man, a chosen man. I must come in from the desert. I must go down among them, if not to be found out, at least to lead by example. I promise. I promise. I promise. I go down on my knees and lift my hands to my face. Show me the way. I am yours to lead. Show me the way. I bow my head and close my eyes. I feel my tear ducts quivering, trying to pull fluid out of my dehydrated body. I decide to lie down. I will receive you lying down. Please. Please. Please.

Thlunk.

I freeze.

Thlunk. Thlunk.

Something is moving upstairs.

Thlunk. Thlunk. Thlunk. Thlunk. Thlunk.

Someone is walking in the ballroom.

■ 14

Someone has just walked across the floor above me. There has been no sound for about ten minutes. If that was a cop up there then he's just discovered a pile of homicide. He'd leave right away, I think. He'd go back to his cruiser and call for backup. That must be where he is. Why did I leave them there? Why didn't I just bury them in the backyard or something? It might have been a neighbour. Someone from church. The pastor, even. Somebody looking for them. I bet that's it.

Thtift. Thtift. Thtift.

Somebody is definitely up there. Someone in the kitchen. I move noiselessly to the bottom of the stairs. There's a hammer on a toolbox. This time I have to. This time it's a chess move. I put my foot carefully on the first step and ease my weight down. I proceed like this, like a cat, until I can see into the hall. I listen. Nothing. I move toward the kitchen with my back to the wall. I hold the hammer up across my chest ready to strike. There's no one in the kitchen. Backing up I manoeuvre myself so I can see as much of the ballroom as possible without losing sight of the front door and the stairs going up. I stand still. My ears adjust and feel like they're moving, looking for sound. I think that death syrup in the air that I've been inhaling has shut down my sense of smell and improved my hearing. I hear the clock in the upstairs kitchen. If I can hear that then I can hear everything. There is no sound. No movement in this house. After a while I advance, first into the ballroom, then the master bedroom, then upstairs. I come down less guarded. There is no one in this house. I return to the ballroom and stand over the sleeping bags. What had I heard? Did I imagine it? I really don't think so. Could it have been an animal? That must be it. Somewhere in the walls. A raccoon maybe. And my mind heard it as footsteps. That has to be it. I definitely heard something but I don't think it was what I thought it was. In any case, it's time to bury the dead. I set the hammer down softly and lean it against the wall. Keep the handle up and ready. Now we scout locations.

The ground in the back yard is hard packed. I find a shovel in a shed. A spade with a repurposed broom handle. The ground is just too hard though, and the broom handle breaks and I manage to remove only a teacup full of hard dirt. I have to put several hundred pounds of people under there somehow. I look up to the top floor. There's a window in the upstairs kitchen that's taller than wide. If I could get the grandmother through and out onto the roof I could roll her down. But that isn't going to get her underground, either. I stand, thinking, with my chin on my hands folded over the top of the broom stick when all of a sudden my nose comes back to life. The death molecules sitting up there must have fallen out and now I smell again. Fresh air. I close my eyes and feel the front of my brain prickle to life. That's what I need. I inhale deeply through my nose. Lilacs. Cedar. Corn. And something sweeter. Something warmer. I open my eyes. Compost. The oxygen shakes each particle of death clear.

The grandmother's bloated body has bloated. I can tell just by looking at her. The skin on her face is pulled taut and ballooning. Her gut has turned from doughy flab into something risen. And the smell. Now that days of death have fallen from my nose I have had to protect it. I daub some VapoRub onto a rag and tie it around the lower part of my face. I have made myself ready to move corpses today. There's a long thin bread knife in a drawer. I make a quick jab in her side just to see what happens. Gases whistle through the pursed lips just below her ribs. I go to the other side and stab a little deeper. It's a bigger sound. Like a whoopee cushion. And the rushing gases push yellow sacs of fat out that collect and run down her side. I hit a few more times in a circle as the hissing belly slowly flattens. It's probably a good thing I did this. She may have exploded when she hit the ground. I continue with some other test stabs. The eyes just roll to the side and back of the sockets. The arms and legs don't bleed. I drive through the bullfrog bloat of her throat and release a torrent of foam and bubbly fluid. I think that's enough. I tie one end of a rope under her arms and roll the other end through the window, letting it fall down the roof and over the gutter.

By the time I've wedged the body into the window I am wearing a thick suit of the indescribable muck that has fallen out of her. As I stand here in the yard with the rope in my gut-greasy palms there are millions of ecstatic flies burrowing and spinning on the extra layer of body sitting on top of my clothes. I draw the rope taut but can't keep my grip. I try wrapping the rope around my wrists but it just slithers free the second I yank. Even if I were to clean my hands or wear gloves the rope is now completely infused with heavy yellow subcutaneous paste. I step back to get a better view when I think I see a shadow move behind the body. In the kitchen, a shadow moves across the wall. I've been like this ever since hearing those noises. I even thought I heard a voice. While I was coming down the stairs. It's not hard to explain though. I'm no fool. I am in a frame of mind that conjures conjurations. I have probably been in that frame of mind for longer than I'm aware of. But I am aware now and the way to answer a conjuring mind is to focus and work. The body has to come down and then the sleeping bags must join her. And if I stand around blinking at every little shadow that talks back then nothing will get done.

A shattering. A bomb has gone off. Shingles and dust and wood spread around me in a cloud. The body has leapt! She leapt! The wind carries the dust away and there she is, not quite all the way to the ground, but close.

She has jumped and caved in the roof. The legs stick out from the V in the wall where she's driven the roof down. I'm suddenly dancing. Suddenly happy. I reach out and grab an ankle. So handy now! I pull and swing the leg free at the knee. I toss it toward the wheelbarrow. The other leg, too. And this is how I get her out of the collapsed rafters. Piecemeal. Her body is shattered and broken and as easy to pull apart as a roasted chicken. The last piece, her head, has fallen into the insulation and I have to get at it through the ceiling above the washing machine, but it's a minor problem. Soon I have all of her tucked and folded into the compost. There are buckets of dissolved tissue splashed across everything back here and the flies are so thick they have formed a chain mail suit over my entire body. But I have done the hardest part. I look back up to the window where she leapt from. She didn't leap. Don't act crazier than you are. Dead bodies don't leap. I watch the window for a moment. Then how did she get down?

■ 15

I am listening a little more than I was before.
Moving more carefully. When it's possible that
your mind is broken it's very important that
you get a fix on the nature of that break. You
have to develop a second mind to watch the
first one. The first one is broken but it's still
possible to cobble together a reliable coalition
as long as you can hold what *isn't* apart from
what *is*. I don't believe I have heard voices.
In fact, I know I haven't, other than catching
myself talking, but that's just garden variety
crazy, not full blown the dog-is-giving-me-
instructions type schizo. I don't think I've
hallucinated things either. I have had some
wound-up moments where my thinking has
broken its pace, but I suspect I may have
allowed that. I have not eaten or slept well

so there have been some delusions and even some nearly psychotic *episodes*. But isn't that all pretty normal given where I'm at? What I've been through? Oh, I think my first mind is broken and not reliable, but that is mostly damage I've caused it and not from some internal defect. My second mind, which I have more or less moved into for the time being, is clearly rational and, because new, undamaged. I do not know how that woman's body got through that window and over the roof. That's the truth and mystery of that. I have to get the rest of these bodies out and into the compost.

I prop the kitchen door open. The bodies have their own little carry bags. And the route is conveniently marked by a wide red line. I will clean up outside when I'm done. Or not. Let the sun and the flies and the creatures of the night suck the pudding up until they're full. That's what I'll do. I grab the first bag and pull. It's light. I don't think of them as the family any more. They aren't. They just are not. The second bag is heavy; the third, somewhere in between. I have stopped smelling again and lost my rag, but here and there I feel a gag in my throat. My sinuses must have stalagmites of rotting flesh. Post-nasal death drip. I swing the third up onto the pile. After each bag I pull material from one of the other compost piles and spread it over. The fourth bag I lay to the side. I don't want the pile to be too tall. There is a compost mound on either side of my bags so I push an entire mound over the fourth bag and sort of feather it up to the top. I'll do the same on the other side with the final bag. I am beginning to feel lighter now. Clearer. My second mind asks if that's a damaged or undamaged way to feel. My first mind says, sometimes it's best to just feel good when you feel good. My second mind sees the benefit.

The last bag is empty.

■ 16

The last sleeping bag is empty.

■ 17

There had been a body in there because the entire upper half of the inside is like lasagna. But now, the bag is empty. Someone has snuck in and removed a body. Just one. Not the other bodies. They have taken just this one body. And because I didn't look—didn't think I needed to—I don't even know which body. Why is there a body missing? I can't even think. I have gone completely ice cold. Who sneaks into a scene like this and steals a corpse? There is no way to know what has happened here. The first mind and the second mind are suddenly on equal footing. The footsteps I heard. Someone had come in. Someone had come in and slid a decomposing body out of a sleeping bag, one of five that lay there, and they snuck away. I don't believe it.

I don't think so. Maybe one of them wasn't dead. Maybe they were just unconscious then woke up and . . . no, that didn't happen. There are bits of skull and brain on the fabric.

Music from somewhere. Loud music from somewhere in house. I nearly fall over. It's not religious music. I stagger back in to the hall. I am being driven mad. I close my eyes and try to wake up somewhere else. In the cornfield. I've fallen asleep covered with husks. I am dreaming. I open my eyes and see myself in a mirror in the hall. Someone is playing music upstairs. No. I close my eyes. I have fallen asleep behind the cash. No woman at the lights. Who kills people for no reason? Not me. Ever. No woman in a van. No cop. No family. I have never and would never kill a soul. In fact, in fact, I am someone you might go to if this were happening. I'm a comfort. I am a comfort! The music is loud. What is scaring me is that whoever is playing the music doesn't even care that I can hear them. Somebody has dragged a body upstairs and is blaring music waiting for me. I have walked into somebody else's trap now. This has been somebody else's trap all along. My minds are tumbling, hitting each other. It is not me that is crazy. It isn't me. Clearly the entirety of everything has flipped out of its hinges or some person, some lone soul, has led me to this point. I have to find out. I have to face this down.

Wind whips down the stairs from the broken window in the kitchen up there. I breathe it deeply as I ascend. Breathing will make me stronger. The music is coming from the other end of the squat hallway that comes off the apartment. There's a door. I walk up and stand inches away. I put my hand on the cheap gessoed wood. The bass bumps across my thumb. This is my house. I make a fist and bang the door.

The music gets louder.

I bang again and feel an anger rising.

The music gets louder. The sound is blown out.

"Turn that off!"

I can hear my voice. It is clear and strong but overpowered.

"Come out here now!"

I beat the door. I kick the door.

"This is my house!"

I realize as I say it that it's not true, but the thought that it could be anyone else's house fills me with real rage.

And then the music stops. I'm about to punch the door and the sound stops. There is a ringing that dies down and then it is completely silent.

"Thank you."

I put my hand over the doorknob.

"I'm coming in now."

The door is locked. I kick the base of the door four times in rapid succession.

"Come out of there! Come out of there!"

I am going to lose control so I step back into the hall, into the breeze from the broken window. I breathe in and out and soon I am calm again. At least I have located the person. In fact, I have them in a cage. I have no idea who they are or why they've done this but it is them trapped in there not me. I have to stay in control.

I walk around the outside of the house looking for a window to the room up there. It sits to the south off the hallway leading off the kitchen. I haven't been there yet. To the front of the house. The driveway. A garage. Yeah, that's right. Takes you five days to locate the getaway car. Anyway, it's too late for that now. I back up in the driveway and scan the roof. There's a small window, a dormer window. I don't think you could climb out of there. It's very narrow. Nobody could get through there. This person is trapped. I have to get back and guard the stairs. I find a long metal bar sitting upright in a pile of loose rocks. I will wait out this madman and I will brain him at the bottom of the stairs.

■ 18

I don't dream while I sleep at the bottom of the stairs. I don't let go of my iron bar. I roll to the side and spend the night snoring into the baseboards. I sleep and I sleep and I sleep. It is the first real sleep I have had in days and nights. It feels as if some merciful hand has laid me down and pushed the world aside so I could sleep. I wake slowly. The bar is against my face on the floor and I smell iron as I blink. I come up on my elbow and am looking at an exposed outlet. There is a dead mouse in the back of the housing. I sit up quickly. Toast. I smell toast. I hold the bar up. There are wet footprints coming down the stairs leading to the kitchen.

In the kitchen the bread sits on the table. The butter and a knife. There is a dish in the sink. I turn and run up the stairs. The door is open and I enter with my weapon up high. Nobody. It's a teenage girl's room. Another door is open behind the bed. A bathroom. I ferret my way to the door and lean in. The shower stall is steamed up. There is a damp towel on the floor.

The phone is ringing. It rings four times and stops. There is a phone up here somewhere.

It rings again. He's calling me. This son of bitch has managed to get out of the house and is calling to taunt me.

I pick up the phone and say nothing.

"Hello?"

I listen. Not a crazy voice.

"Hello?"

I answer.

"Yes?"

"Mr. Lerner?"

I turn and back into the wall. This isn't going to be what I thought.

"Uh. Yes."

I cough, correcting my voice a little.

"Mr. Lerner. Good morning. It's Charlie Baker from DSS. I'm Patty's art teacher. We've never spoken."

"Good morning, Mr. Baker. Yes. Is there a problem?"

I try to think of why she's not in school. Keep it simple. She has the flu. We all do. The doctor said to just hole up in the house till everyone's in the clear.

"Well, Mr. . . . . Jeffrey, can I call you Jeffrey?"

"Yes, that's fine."

"I have Patty here right now and it appears she might have fallen down or something on her way to school. She has a nasty cut above her nose and, well, it's quite a gash."

I feel the phone slipping. I have to turn into the wall to keep it in my hand.

"Anyway, yeah, she seems a little worse for wear, sir. I think she needs to see a doctor right away. In fact, I almost called an ambulance when I first saw her."

I mouth a word but still feel like I might fall down.

"But she's otherwise okay. A little out of it but you know teenagers. So, we're just going to send her on home, I think. For the day. But, like I say, you might want to get her looked at."

I have slid down the wall to the floor.

"Will you or your wife be at home?"

"Yes."

"Okay. Good. Thanks, Jeffrey. I'm sure she's fine."

"Okay. I'm sure, too. Thanks. Bye."

■ 19

First things first. I stand at the door in the kitchen leading out back. I am not looking out yet. I don't really expect to see them all standing up in the compost but I have to eliminate the possibility. Mr. Baker has put a whole new stamp on this. I do not yet know what I'm dealing with but it isn't pictures on the roof of my skull. I turn and open the door.

Vultures. There are a dozen massive black vultures on the mound. They hear me and roll their tiny crimson faces to me. Their wings reach up all across the yard like an army waving black death flags. Vultures. Their feet are deep in faces and ribs and pelvises. They are not scared. They are many. I hear a low growl and look down. Maggots roil around on every surface; in fact, they *are* a surface. A shivering skin of dazzling detail that moves across everything. And the shadow of a dog. Two dogs. More. I see them lunging just before I close the door. The beasts hurl their weight and the door heaves in. I push back but it doesn't close. A set of sharp grinning teeth poking out from under the door. Then other mouths stab in along the door's edge. I push hard and the growls deepen. I feel weight against the door. Some of these dogs must be as heavy as men. I cannot hold them. I launch myself and dive to the door beside the fridge. The dogs don't follow immediately, a bit stunned at falling so suddenly into the room. I make it though and manage to close the door before they assault it. I run to the basement and find the hammer. There's a small workbench screwed to the wall with cans of nails on it. I pull books from a shelf, Bibles and heavy volumes of accounting texts. The planks from the shelf are thick and dense. I nail them in with the longest spikes I can find. One across each corner of the door. All this time the dogs are exploding, tearing the kitchen apart and slamming into the door. I check the front door to make sure it's closed and I return to the basement to check that it too is secure. There is a sizable part of hell outside trying to get in. I go to the kitchen upstairs and stand in the shattered window above the collapsed section of roof.

The vultures are mingling on the mound and give the appearance of a single black creature. Occasionally a pink head snaps up to swallow organ meat in a single repulsive spasm. From here I can't see the maggots moving but I know they are there. The ground that looks still from up here is actually marching across itself with a billion pumping bodies. The first dog comes out and makes a short run at the vultures. Broad black wings shoot up and form a wall decorated obscenely with pinkish-purple heads. The dog backs down, but another appears. And another. Soon all of the dogs, maybe eight or ten of them, form a line facing the birds. The vultures seem to know how to share death and they drift off the top of the mound, letting the dogs in.

I return to the now peaceful main floor. It seems I am, remarkably, looking forward to Patty coming home.

■ 20

I don't have to wait long. I hear the front door
open. I stay seated, listening, as she opens the
closet door and hangs up her coat. I hear a sigh
as one boot comes off. Then the other. I even
hear the light pat of her stocking feet down the
hall as she approaches. I try to make myself
as ready as possible, breathing in deeply and
exhaling slowly. She sits beside me. I glance at
her knees. Heavy black stockings and tartan
skirt. Catholic school. She extends her feet
and points her toes then swings her legs back
under the settee.

"I'm sorry about the music."

I look over. She's pretty. About fifteen.
There is a massive hole in the centre of her
forehead and her eyes are encircled with
heavy shades of black and deep purple. There

are small delicate red spiders of burst blood vessels on her cheeks.

"That's okay. I'm sorry I kicked your door."

She shrugs and brings a hand up to her forehead.

"Does that hurt?"

She pushes the edge of the hole.

"No."

I lower my head. There is no question that she is here.

"Do you want an aspirin or something?"

She shakes her hair down over her face.

"No. I'm fine. Can I just go to my room?"

I think it would be very small of me to wonder why we have roles at this point.

"Yes."

She shifts forward and stands.

"I won't play loud music."

She doesn't look at me. It seems we are shy.

"It's okay. You do what you want."

She leaves and heads for the stairs. I rise without thinking.

"Patty?"

She stops and turns without looking up.

"I'm sorry."

Her head tilts and she looks out between two bands of hair.

"What I did, I mean."

Patty sidesteps so she's half hidden by the archway. She takes hair in her hand and pulls it across her chin.

"I know. It sucks pretty bad."

I don't know what to say. I think I should say nothing. Patty takes a step back and turns toward the stairs.

"I don't know what to say."

I'm at the bottom of the stairs and Patty stops halfway up. She thinks for moment then looks back.

"I miss my little brother."

I see my fingers shaking on the banister.

"That's all. I miss him."

Patty looks at my hand then moves the hair from her face.

"You don't have to say anything."

She sighs. She wants to go.

"Patty?"

"Yes?"

"I don't know why."

"You don't know why what?"

"I didn't have to. I just did it. I don't know why."

There. I said it. It's true. I don't know why.

"I'm going to go lay down now."

I wait until I hear her door close before I move.

Night falls at around seven and I don't get off the settee or turn any lights on until eight. I stand by the barricaded kitchen door and listen. There are animals in there rooting around and I hear the occasional screech of a vulture. They are still feeding. It occurs to me that Patty hasn't had any dinner but I think it's more important that she rests. I am tired too. I haven't managed to ask myself why she's here because I am drained and worn and beaten. I am going to sleep in a bed tonight. I am going to put my head on a pillow.

DING.

Someone is at the door.

DING.

I can't do this now.

DING.

A bald man with round glasses dressed entirely in black. A black turtleneck.

"Hello, Mr. Lerner. Charlie Baker."

He extends a hand and I shake it. I don't know what I look like.

"Can I come in for a second?"

I draw the door and let him by. We stand in the alcove looking at each for a moment. I don't think I'll bring him right into the house. I really don't want to kill Charlie Baker. He has a friendly face.

"Well, how is she?"

I don't close the door completely. I want Charlie Baker to escape.

"She seems okay. She says she's fine."

Charlie nods. He's heard this from her, too, but still something's bothering him.

"It's just, that's a helluva . . . helluva big gash she's got there. And she wouldn't say how she got it. How'd she get that, Mr. Lerner?"

I widen my eyes, thinking. You need to accept what I say, Mr. Baker. Your life depends on it.

"She fell. In the morning. She was running down the basement steps and she tripped and this bar . . . a rebar caught her right between the eyebrows up here."

I point to the spot. Charlie Baker stares hard at me for a second, then whistles.

"Well, holy shit, Mr. Lerner. Holy shit. She's lucky she didn't lose an eye. Or worse."

I nod repeatedly.

"Yes. Oh. She scared me pretty good."

"But she's okay now?"

"Seems to be."

"You don't think she needs to see a doctor?"

I make a parent face. Weighing the practicals.

"I think it looks a lot worse than it is."

Charlie Baker gives me another study. It still bothers him.

"Patty told us your wife took the other kids to the States for a couple weeks. Relatives?"

"Uh. Yeah. My sister."

Charlie moves sideways. He's going to leave soon.

"Okay. That's fine, but in the future could you give us a little heads-up when you plan to pull the kids from school for that long? We don't mind but we like to send them off with some homework so they don't get too behind."

"Oh, sure. Sorry."

Charlie Baker fixes on me again. This is almost good enough for him but still not quite. He lingers, trying to think of the question that might get the answer he's looking for.

"Okay, Mr. Lerner. Well, tell Patty I hope she feels better."

I match steps with him as he moves through the door.

"Will do, Mr. Baker."

"Call me Charlie."

"Sure, Charlie. Thanks for dropping by."

Charlie Baker pulls a knitted black cap on top of his bald head and heads up the long dark driveway. I hear the dogs and vultures wrestling and grunting at the side of the house. This was a dangerous thing for you to do, Charlie.

■ 21

I make breakfast in the upstairs kitchen while Patty showers. The downstairs kitchen is still a barricaded portal to hell. I got up early and mopped the floor but there's nothing I can do about the shattered window and splintered frame. I did remove the tags of skin and flesh but there are still ruddy marks against the wall and on the sill. I hope she doesn't look out because the birds are still eating her family.

I set the table for two. Toast and jam, eggs and sausage. I manage coffee but can't find any juice. When she appears I stand in front of the massive hole. I hope she can pretend it's not there. I decide to let her speak first.

"Morning."

"Morning, Patty. I made some breakfast. Do you eat breakfast?"

She sits and looks at her plate.

"Looks good."

I sit without taking my eyes off her. The hole in her forehead isn't closing or healing, but it isn't festering either. Her eyes are shaded prettily in blue and purple. Bruises that haven't changed. She pulls her long black hair back behind her shoulders.

"There's a breeze in here."

I reach across and pour her coffee.

"Are you cold?"

She peers in the cup and pours in sugar straight from the bowl.

"No. I'm fine. It's nice."

She sips her coffee and looks past me to the window.

"Something happened there."

I turn to look as if just noticing.

"Yeah. Sorry. That's my fault. You don't really want to know."

"I guess I don't."

She sips silently, staring out the window.

"Your eggs'll get cold."

It takes her a while to respond. She puts the cup down.

"She made a smell up here."

I don't say anything. She means her grandmother.

"The whole floor started to smell the moment she moved in."

I take a butter of toast. The death odour is still here but diffused by fresh air blowing through the hole.

"Better now."

A dog snaps at another. A low growl. Patty picks up a sausage. Her fingers are fish-belly white.

"I'm going to the movies after school with Jesse."

I hear scraping on the ground outside. A grackle calls in its cleated voice.

"Okay. You feel okay to go to school?"

Patty isn't going to eat.

"Yeah. I'm going. It's okay if I go to the movies with Jesse?"

I shrug.

"I don't think it'd be smart to bring him home though."

Patty laughs. It's a shocking sound. I didn't expect to hear laughter. Really, I didn't expect to hear laughter for the rest of my life.

"What's so funny?"

"Oh. That's what my mom used to say too. For very different reasons."

I pour Patty some more coffee.

"She didn't like him much. She'd never let me just go off to the movies with him. Or anything."

She pours the sugar. She has a wry smile. She's an intelligent person.

"Where's your dad?"

Patty puts the sugar bowl down hard enough to raise a chorus of barks from outside.

"That's a stupid question. Let's not just get fuckin' stupid. Okay?"

That she's angry is almost too much. I hold the edge of the table and have to concentrate to not cry.

"I'm sorry. I'm sorry. I won't ask."

She looks fiercely into my eyes. She has violence in her.

"I'm done anyway."

I am forced to look down. I can't speak as she pushes the chair back and leaves. The sound of the chair across the floor triggers a fight between dog and vulture. Patty closes the door to her room. I collect the dishes, slide the food off them and lay them in the sink to clean later. The cackling and snapping subsides and I lean through the hole. Flies are being born. There's a black haze drifting close to the ground. It is agitating the dogs that snap madly into the infuriating cloud.

"Okay. I'm going."

Patty has a backpack over one shoulder. Her black hair is once again hiding her face.

"Okay. Look . . . I'm—"

She interrupts.

"No. I'm sorry. You just wanted to know. I'm sorry. I can be a bit . . ."

She rolls her eyes and points to her temple.

"Sometimes. I'm sorry. He left."

I nod. I didn't really need to know. It was a stupid question.

"Mom stopped going to church and started drinking. So he said he was going to let her take us all to hell and then . . . he left."

I make a sympathetic noise in my throat.

"Charlie Baker thinks he's still here."

She laughs again. It is a perfect sound.

"Well, what Charlie Baker doesn't know can't hurt him."

It's a strange conspiratorial thing to say. I laugh. This time *I* laugh.

■ 22

Patty left to catch the school bus at a quarter of nine. I found myself wandering through the house feeling excited. I tidied and mopped and swept and cleaned. I straightened pictures, pictures of people I had killed, yes—but now they were just pictures, crooked and made straight as I strolled along each wall. I can't say I know what is happening to me here or how, but Patty, beautiful, sad and bruise-coloured Patty, has decided all on her own that I am here and that I will help her. And it's not like I haven't done the things I've done. To her and her family. We both know exactly. We were both here when it happened. And it's certainly not that I am making it up to her. How can I? It can't be done. It's just this: we are magical. She must know this. We are magical. An intensity

166

of experience has transformed us into beings that circle above fear and doubt and pain.

I break from cleaning to eat lunch. Food is starting get scarce and I don't know if there's any money in the house. Patty will help with that. I open a can of beans and heat it in a too-big iron pot. I eat by the window, enjoying the breeze. Even the dogs yelping and snarling are mine today. I lean out the window.

"Hey! Quiet!"

They stop and look up. There are fewer vultures and I catch myself thinking I need to fill the bird feeder.

After lunch I consider calling the school and asking Charlie Baker how our Patty's faring today. It wouldn't be totally out of the picture. I may later.

I find myself with nothing to do in the afternoon and I wander past Patty's bedroom door. I hover for a moment, wondering if I should.

It seems a typical teenage girl's room. A movie poster. Some dark pencil sketches of skinny children. No computer. A small stereo that plays cassettes. Books in a row on the floor against the wall beside her bed. I pull the sheets and covers up, smoothing and tucking them under the mattress. I decide that's what I'm doing here. I'm making her bed.

That night she comes home before dinner. She runs through the front door and straight up the stairs. She leaves the door wide open and stomps upstairs with her boots still on. Something bad has happened. I look up the driveway before I close the door. If someone was coming behind her . . . Jesse. Or Charlie. Or the police. Something bad has happened. I realize that this is one of those moments when I should respect her privacy. I should accept that had she wanted to talk to me she would have, but the stakes are too high. She is out there in the world and anything could happen.

"Patty?"

She turns her music on loud. She doesn't want to talk. I am tempted to go up and try but I can't risk her being angry with me. Patty could do great damage to me. It's an awful feeling and I am desperate to know but I step back and into the hall to wait. All of the magic I felt today is replaced by anxiety. Dread. I think I should do something. Keep myself occupied, but there isn't anything left to do. And I'm too upset. I have to talk to Patty. I sit and wait. I sat here once for sixteen hours in far worse condition. It was a holding cell I made for myself to live in instead of dying. Things were simpler then. I watch dusk fall across the windows and my reflection slowly develop like a picture on the black. My hair is sticking straight up and I have a short beard. Charlie Baker mustn't be a very judgemental person. The music is turned down and then off. I don't move for a while. She may come down. She may feel like talking now. I'm glad I left her alone. It was the right decision.

I'm not sure how much time has passed but it seems pretty clear that she isn't coming. I rise on stiff legs and walk, head bowed, to the bottom of those terrible stairs again.

I call softly.

"Patty?"

I listen and consider climbing up to her.

"Patty?"

I hear her door open and seconds later she appears. She descends without a word, without looking at me and she passes me. I don't move, letting her go where she wants. Waiting for her to be there so I can turn.

I sit beside her on the settee.

"Do you want to talk about it?"

She is sniffling. She's been crying. I reach up and draw the hair back from her face. She lets me tuck it behind her ear.

"I get worried."

She turns to me. Her eyes are wet and swollen. The bruises looking like heavy makeup running in her tears.

"Jesse's an asshole."

I feel guilty for being relieved.

"Why? What did Jesse do?"

Patty looks squarely at me. Her eyes wander up into my hair. She laughs and wipes her nose.

"You look like a freak right now."

I turn to my reflection and try pulling my hair down.

"I know. I know. I've let myself go."

She stops laughing and wipes her eyes with the backs of her hands. Her laugh has made me feel selfish.

"Jesse is an asshole because he ignored me all day and hid with his asshole friends and never once talked to me."

I put my arm around her. She leans into me.

"He acted like I wasn't even there."

This alarms me.

"But he's wrong. You were there. Mr. Baker even said so."

She pulls away and gives me a look.

"Don't be a weirdo."

I return her look with a guilty-as-charged face.

"Look, boys Jesse's age are still trying to figure out if they think with the pack or on their own. And that pack is pretty powerful. Some people never leave it."

She smiles. She thinks I'm right.

"And some of us never even figure out where the pack is."

Patty nods, grinning. Those lovely conspiracy eyes again. There are bright red patterns at the edges of the dark purple on her cheeks that I never noticed before. She has the most interesting face in the world.

"Are you trying to give me wisdom now?"

I put my hand to my mouth.

"Wisdom?"

"Yeah. Your fuckin' wisdom."

I feign for her.

"I don't think so. Was that wisdom?"

She bumps her shoulder to mine.

"Not even close."

We don't need Jesse. If Jesse wants to pretend that Patty's not there then it's a great loss to his world.

■ 23

I didn't bother making dinner for us tonight. Patty said she wasn't hungry and I just made a quick sandwich while she read in her room. I went to look for the television but remembered I had thrown it out in pieces earlier today. I thought about going up and borrowing one of Patty's books but that might just seem like pandering. I have to be aware of doing my own things in this house. I don't need to climb up into everything she does. I decide to sit at the dining room table and make a list. There are things that have to be sorted out. Mail, for instance. There's a post office box somewhere, probably in New Lowell, that's going to get very stuffed if we don't figure out how to clean it out. I pull drawers, looking for keys. I find an inordinate amount of candles and batteries but no keys. I wander through the house looking for a nail or something where they might hang. I find it at the front door. Several rings, in fact. Car keys. I tuck them in my pants pocket. I have had a vague scenario playing in the back of my mind where Patty and I take a trip up north and never return. It's a simple, attractive idea, but without money or cover it's just a live-happily-ever-after kind of fantasy. As much as I want things to continue I know what this will mean depends on the right ending. I find the mailbox key. It doesn't feel very good in my hand. None of the letters will be meant for me to open. Probably none for Patty, either. It may be a connection we shouldn't tug at.

I used to have trouble around people. All of my life I had trouble. I struggled to know what to say. I would get dizzy and my head would shatter to pieces. And that's what happened to me. It's not much of an explanation and I have to say that I can't really remember the feeling any more. That morning in Cashtown Corners seems so unreal to me now. It felt unreal then too, I'm sure, but now that I seem to be looking after things, saying the right things, thinking clearer, those monstrous events *must* have happened to another person. Is that possible? I am *not* him any more. I am who I am now. I should try to keep in mind that it wasn't always this way. It could change again.

Patty has read herself to sleep and I look in on her. Her large black boots sit in the middle of the floor. I'll leave them until tomorrow. At least she changed out of her clothes before she went to bed. I move silently forward and turn the bedside light off. A soft blue night light ticks on beside her row of books. This light makes her face glow like a pearl.

The next morning, after Patty gets on the school bus, I decide it's time to do something about the beasts on the hill. I need a weapon and it occurs to me that there may be more ammunition for that old pistol. I stop myself though. I don't think I could bring myself to holding that thing again. Let alone pointing it. Shooting it. I don't really want anything to do with the iron bar, either. Or the little wooden bat. Especially the little wooden bat. So I search the laundry room for poison and I find a large white jug of pure bleach. I may not kill them with it but if I manage to soak the mound in bleach then maybe they'll move on. I put my ear to the kitchen door. I don't hear anything but I'm not going to go through there. They could be crouching on the floor, silent and listening too. I'll sneak around the side of the house.

I enter the garage for the first time. There's a minivan sitting in the dark. A stack of bagged winter tires. A generator. I find a long-handled axe and swing it by my feet. It's too heavy to bring up easily in one hand. I could throw the bottle of bleach to the mound, then hack my way through the dogs to it. I am going to get hurt, I'm pretty sure of that. Something will get to me along the way. But if I manage to kill even one then maybe the rest will back off. The vultures should just take wing. They won't fight me. That's not what they do. Vultures attack with patience. They'll fly off and wait until I kill the dogs and go back inside. Then they collect in the sky out of nowhere and descend on the mound. And then the bleach will dissolve their hideous faces. It seems to me that I have a plan.

I test my balance with the two objects before turning the corner. They are about equal weight but I have to be careful not to lose my balance when I launch the bottle. It has to be a clean throw and I have to come out of it with a flying edge. I have to take something out with that first chop, which means I'll have to be swinging on the run.

I pump my knees once to feel them spring then turn the corner with a howl. I toss the bleach with a deep underhand throw and it goes high, end over end. Then I spin the butt of the handle into that hand as it comes down and I manage to draw it back far behind me before driving it forward and down, looking for a dog to hit. The axe head slams into the ground and sends a shock wave up my arms that nearly pops my shoulder out. There is no dog. There are no dogs. I look across the yard to the mound. The bleach bottle sits upright near the top. No vultures. No flies. There is a strange supernatural gleam to the entire scene. They have eaten and chewed and licked and sucked every last molecule of human remains. The dogs have even dragged off the bones and probably buried them in the cornfield. The mound has been restored to a clean black oven. But it's the shine that takes my breath away, white barely there frost that sparkles on everything. This is the dried spit of flies. The light dust left when the sun evaporates maggot saliva. I step around the axe and turn in slow circles. Even the crushed roof has a sparkling finish and the garden wall has been polished, its stones glowing like large misshapen pearls. As I move my eyes across the surfaces, shimmering bolts appear and disappear in the air. I breathe deep and an acrid but pleasing dust lines the inside of my nose. Tonight, Patty, we will sit out here, with

the crazy stars above us and the magic stars
here, below.

■ 24

The downstairs kitchen is sterile and polished in the same way as the yard, but it's no longer serviceable. There is nothing in the pantry. All of the cords are missing. Anything that simply sat on a counter is gone. It's not a room any longer. Now it resembles the inside of a bleached skull. I lean into the door to see if I can loosen the planks from in here. I bounce my shoulder into the immovable panel. I secured it very well, it seems. I consider getting the axe and splitting my way through. When you've had an axe in your hands and readied yourself to use it, the feeling lingers for a while. Lazy though, and it would be a shame to make a mess of such a pristine room. Even the insides of the cupboards look resurfaced. And then I spot something interesting. Two china white cups sitting on the window sill. The only loose objects left. I pick them up and realize that these aren't cups. These are parts of skulls. The edges are irregular but smooth and it's as if they've been kiln fired and enamelled. There is something in the spit of maggots and the shit of flies and the drool of mad dogs that, when combined and worked in with rough tongues and brushed with scrubbing bodies, becomes a kind of super surface. I set the skull caps down on the counter and marvel at how continuous the effect of this sheen is. From the drawer handles to the weeds at the back door, everything is held in a perfect frost.

I walk carefully through the garden and around to the front door. I wish I could see more from here. Only the road leading up across the corn field. Beyond that just the endless sea. Somewhere over there, in a hidden crease, sits Cashtown Corners. There must be people not too far from where I'm standing right now who are busy hunting for me. I am a missing person. Not a wanted man, but a victim, unaccounted for, probably lying in a shallow grave with a cleaver in my face. The last missing piece in a crime adventure that has gripped the nation. And that boy, the pump jockey turned angel of death, Jeremy what's-his-name, is still hanging grimly onto the facts while we ask our questions, all we want, all the people want, is to know, what have you done with the body of Mr. Clark, you greedy, evil little monster?

I really have nothing to do but am nervous about being bored. I remember those hours and days in Cashtown. That was the ocean that first pulled me away. I will make Patty's bed. I may even wash her sheets. Maybe there's other laundry I can do.

She has made the bed herself and I admit to feeling a bit slighted by this. I don't mind, Patty. Let me do the things I like to do. But, she may have just thought she was being a good girl. How many teenagers make their beds before going off to school? I poke around looking for clothes I can clean and manage a small pile of socks and tee shirts. I straighten the tie-dyed doily on her bedside table and notice that it isn't a table at all. It's a small television set. I turn it to face out and carefully flip the doily up. My heart starts to bang up against my throat. Should I turn it on? I've settled the story for myself. Do I need it contradicted? Do I really need to know? I press the power button and a green diamond winks at me from the centre of the screen. A bass beat erupts from the side speakers seconds before an image brightens the screen. A music video channel. A man sits on a yacht being driven by three women. I feel around the folded doily and find the remote. I begin to move up from this channel. 24 is sports. A golf tournament. 25 is CNN. I stop here. Is Cashtown an international story? Could it be? The anchor sits in front of a graph showing foreclosures rising. 27 is a men's channel. People being knocked into orange water by multicoloured punching gloves. 28 is me.

My face looks back at me. It's a new picture.

They've gone through the trailer. The picture shrinks to one side and the other picture, the one cropped from the Don Cherry photo snaps up beside it. I check the remote and press the volume. There is a man standing in Cashtown Corners. A reporter stands in front of pumps 3 and 4.

"Police are not telling us everything but the prime suspect, the gas jockey who was apprehended fleeing the scene with twelve thousand dollars is now either an accomplice, or a witness, or a victim himself. In any case police are stepping up their hunt for the owner, this man, Bob Clark, and are sending out a nationwide alert to the public to call immediately if they spot him. Police also warn that he may be armed and dangerous. Police are also telling us that they have put in a request to the long-running TV program *America's Most Wanted* for assistance in apprehending Mr. Clark. In spite of the warning that he is a dangerous man police are only saying that he is wanted for questioning."

Charlie Baker. Charlie Baker saw me. I look in the mirror in Patty's bathroom.

I am thinner. I have a beard. I pull my eyes open. They are brown but I detect an orange fleck in there that wasn't there before. My mouth. My eyes. Even with the beard. Even thinner. Even with the orange fleck. I am him. I look exactly like him. Oh Charlie, Charlie, Charlie. But you think I'm Patty's father. I hear him. He says to someone, "You know, that guy that killed all those people looks an awful lot like Patty's father." He might doubt for a moment, the coincidence, then some responds, "But Patty's father isn't Bob Clark, right? I mean, they know the guy they're looking for. They aren't looking for Patty's father." Charlie Baker would have to concede to that. He'd know right then and there that the man who looks like Patty's father is simply someone else. Then he'd reason to himself the other part—*This guy here is heavier, anyway, and clean shaven.*

My heart is punching my chest so hard I

can see my shirt shake. I have to stay fixed on that scenario. It is the most likely and certainly the only way it plays out. But there's something else. Something else. Charlie came around here asking after Patty. He wanted to know what happened to Patty's head. The head I shot. Did he suspect something? How could he? Patty can't be walking around with a bullet hole in her forehead. Suddenly I can't hear Charlie thinking anymore. I can't really say what's going on in there. There are too many variables. The dots are too scribbled around to see their connections. I have to call the school.

"Good morning, Duntroon Secondary."

Nice voice. Good morning. The morning is going good.

"Hi. Could I speak to Charlie Baker, please?"

"I'll check if he's teaching a class."

The line is held. It goes to local news radio. I hear the name Bob Clark and press the phone to my chest. My heart tires to escape through my back so I push the phone against my thigh.

I am convinced that I am going to slip now.
I'm going to say "Hi, Charlie, it's Bob Clark."
In fact, there's a terrible pressure in the back
of my head pushing the name down onto my
tongue. This is what happens when you think
you are thinking clearly when you are not. I
have damaged all my minds now and there is
no time to establish a working one.

"Charlie Baker."

"Hi, Charlie, it's Patty's father."

"Oh, hi. I was going to call you."

"Oh yeah? What were you going to call me
about?"

"Just wanted to check on Patty. How is
she?"

It's almost too normal. I need to confront
facts. I need to refute things.

"She seems a lot better now. How's she
doing in school?"

"Well, Mr. Lerner, to tell you the truth, she
seems a little . . . a little off. I don't know how
to describe it."

I am the thinner, bearded man with an orange fleck in his eye.

"Well try, couldja, Charlie?"

Silence. What tone did I just use? Something went funny there. Charlie coughs.

"Okay. Well, she's really isolated. Just not the same girl. Not eating either."

I hurry to pick up the major points.

"Isolated. That doesn't sound too good. Not eating?"

Silence again. I think I must be coming off wrong here. I should never have called. I need to get out. Now.

"Well, I'm aware that teenagers, especially teenage girls, go through—"

"Uh, oh. Charlie. I gotta go."

"Oh?"

"Yeah. Bye, Charlie."

Phone hangs up. We shared some concerns and then I had to go so we'll just hope for the best and that she's going to be okay. That's where we stand and I'm Patty's dad who is a bit weird to talk to but that doesn't make him a crazy killer on the loose. I should never have called. If he comes around here I know I will kill him. When I squeeze my eyes I see scribbled faces again. I need Patty to come home.

This house is where I made things better. I wander out into the hall. The photos I straightened. This is where I grew up. I put my fingers on the family. I miss them. It's strange how memory attaches itself to things. Memories adrift cling to whatever floats to stay alive. The thing that preserves a memory isn't anything like the memory itself. A smell or a colour or a sound. That row of trees behind Patty in this picture is gone now. We put the wall there instead. I step back from the pictures. I have been talking. It's time to sit on the settee carefully and figure out how we protect Patty.

I have done this before. Discarded myself in order to be here. I have to accept certain things if I am to return properly. First: They are coming to get me. Once I allow that fact then I can begin to make some real final moments possible. They are coming to get me. I have to say something that will help. Like this: You are not going to run. I am not going to run. All the rest of it. The magic. That is coming to an end. My heart is slowing. It doesn't matter what I said to Charlie Baker. It doesn't matter what I remember. I am going to be taken away soon. There are thoughts you can have that actually cause chemicals to be released in your blood that make you feel that everything is okay. And there are thoughts you can have that release chemicals in your blood that tell you that you are going to die. I need to find the thought that releases both. Specific thought, regardless of where it comes from or how it is made true. A simple chain of words and a little bead of plausibility.

A grackle lands in the empty bird feeder, turns twice to defend it, then flies off. I need a thought that has the effect of music. Two finches sneak up from below. They've been pecking seed that has fallen into the grass. Smarter bird. I wonder where the bird feed is. I could fill it. I go down into the basement and root around in the boxes under the stairs. I find a bag of bird feed sitting on a cross stud in the unpanelled wall. I also see a bottle of red wine. I take both.

The front door opens upstairs. No ring. No knock. Just someone walking in. Patty's home early. I am apprehensive. What if her face is scribbled out? What if I go up and I can't even look her in the eye? I return the bag of seed and climb the stairs with the wine.

Patty runs down the hall with her boots on. I look down, afraid as she passes me. I hear that she's crying. I turn to follow. She's on the stairs running up to her room. Part of me wants her to get there. To close the door. I would leave her. I would leave this house. But she stops suddenly halfway up the stairs. I can't look at her. I don't want her face—that beautiful broken face—to be chopped to pieces by the mad lines.

"You know what?"

I don't look to answer.

"What?"

"Everybody can go fuck themselves."

The thought. The chemicals just moved. I look up. It is her face. Tears in black and blue and a slippery smile.

"Yes, they can."

I reach my hand up and she looks at it.

"You can go fuck yourself too."

I nod, accepting this.

She comes down and takes my hand.

"So what are we going to do about it?"

She hooks her arm in mine. I stoop to pick up the wine.

"I am going to pour this wine into your brothers' skulls."

She stops and looks up at me.

"Well, *that's* big."

We reach the barred door and I carefully unhook her arm. I pull on each brace until the nails give up then I put my hand on the doorknob. Patty steps back and raises her hand.

"It's been redone."

We step out into the kitchen and the sun has moved lower in the sky so that the rays are creating colour in the crystal surface. Pink and blue and yellow shapes move in crisp patterns across the floor. Patty gasps. I pick up the skulls and drag two chairs out into the yard. Patty follows, making soft disbelieving sounds. I place the chairs on patio stones that seem iced and powdered like fresh confections. Patty walks out into the yard. She moves slowly, watching how nothing stays still, how even the dirt is luminous now. I let her. This is something I don't think anyone has ever seen before. I open the wine and carefully pour it. I know she is crying. I don't have to look. I am too. It's what we should be doing.

I raise my cup.

"To terrible life."

I hold Patty's cup in an upturned palm and pass it. She accepts demurely.

"To terrible life."

We tilt the bones at our lips and empty them. Patty swallows and coughs.

"Sorry. I don't drink. Not old enough."

I arch my eyebrows. *Scandalous.*

"How was your day?"

I like her asking me this.

"Well. I found this."

I stretch my arm out, presenting the yard again.

"This is something."

I am refilling the cups.

"And I called Charlie Baker."

I drink half in one gulp. Patty keeps hers in her lap.

"Oh. I didn't have his class today. Why did you call him?"

I like wine.

"Oh. Just to see how you were doing."

"Charlie Baker doesn't know."

"I got that. How was your day?"

I refill my cup and watch Patty take a sip. She doesn't swallow.

I put my hand on her knee.

"Are you okay?"

The wine slips from the corners of her mouth. There's something wrong.

"Patty! Oh my god."

It's not wine. It's blood. Blood is running from her nose and her mouth. She grunts and leans forward then snaps her head back. When she speaks there are holes erupting on her chin.

"How many? You cocksucker! How many?"

I don't understand and I'm frightened.

"How many what?"

Three of Patty's teeth have fallen into her hand.

"How many days?"

She coughs and blood comes out in a puff.

"I don't know what . . ."

I extend my hand to catch teeth falling from her chin. She turns to me as her face pulls in at the middle. Her mouth deforms her words now.

"How many days is *today*?"

"How many? How many? My fuckin' God, Patsy, if we knew the answer to that maybe we could get on with this horseshit, and have the proper fucking day we planned to have."

■ 25

I am at the side of the house when Patty comes
home. I hear the door slam shut. Luckily I have
the axe with me and it's just a matter of where's
the best place to surprise her. The downstairs
kitchen would be best but if I start splattering
that door in with an axe she's going to skip out
the front door like Pollyanna. It has to be the
front door. I put the heft of the handle in both
hands and let it pull my muscle. She will die
for sure. The front door is locked so I go to the
tall bay windows at the ballroom. Looks like
it's going to be a splashdown this time. Rear
the axe up so it's directly centred over my head
and I bring it down. The glass and wood rip
like paper and with a quick side to side I get a
hole big enough. Points of glass catch me on
the way through, but that's okay. I was never

going to do this without a little blood of my own. Her music is on and fills the entire upper floor. I'm disappointed for a second. I wanted that to be my entrance, but this will cut out the chance that she might get away. This is the kill that matters. This is the one that didn't stick the first time.

I feel sweat running down one side of my face and from my elbows. I look. It's not sweat, it's blood. I have some deep cuts all through the outline of my body. I come up the stairs slowly. I hear my breath retreating from the music to a dark bladder that palpitates in the middle of my head. I reach the wind from the kitchen and turn to face her door. She has nowhere to go. I am here now. I reach over and softly turn the handle. I'm going to kick it open and fly through.

My foot lands higher on the door than I expect and I have to hop to get my balance back. Patty is lying on her bed, face down, with her arms up under her pillow. Her head lifts slightly to look but the axe comes down like a comet. The blade cracks in halfway down her spine and presses clear through to her stomach. I try to pull it up but it's like a gaffe hook in a big fish. I drag hard, trying to pull her from the room. If I can get her out then I have better swinging options. The axe pops out and I fall. I hold tight, afraid that Patty may not die properly. She is moving but it's a death seizure. Trembles fed by profound neurological damage. She will not live. I send the axe up and down again for good measure and clap the back of her head in half. This is the big success I was looking for. I pause over her for a moment. This is a dead person. I chuck the axe onto the bed. My day ends here.

■ 26

In the morning I hear them coming. They are setting up the perimeter. I see the roofs of cruisers through the trees up the driveway. I watch, hidden, from the upstairs kitchen. They have removed the doubt in Charlie Baker's mind. They helped him get the answer he was looking for. Trees rustle with movement and I even hear the bleating of a radio here and there. These people aren't too worried if I see them coming. They just want to be in the right place no matter what. I turn back into the house, past Patty's room and drop my foot onto the top step. I won't let them shoot me. I realize that I have no interest in dying. I wonder if they'll storm in or call for me on a megaphone. I have to be careful not to surprise anyone. I am calm again and

I have done what I came to do. In the hall I hear them jostling around on the front porch. Probably arguing over who gets to swing the battering ram. I stand far enough back and centre myself. They'll see me in time and I'll lay down when they ask. No stupid squiggle faces. No more fingering loose change in convenience stores. All my little moments are over. It's time to just live my life.

■ ACKNOWLEDGEMENTS

I would like to thank ChiZine Publications for their hard work on this: Brett Savory, Sandra Kasturi, Erik Mohr, C. A. Lewis, Matthew Moore, Helen Marshall, Laura Marshall, Clare Marshall, Samantha Beiko.

Derek McCormack for his thoughtless taunts early on and his thoughtful cleaning later.

Charlie Baker who supplied himself. Ed Gatavackas, Jayde Barlowe, Sophy Pollack, and Jesse Burgess.

■ ABOUT THE AUTHOR

Tony Burgess writes fiction and for film.

He lives in Stayner with his wife, Rachel, and their two children, Griffin and Camille.